Praise for Theodore Carter

"Populated by sideshow fairies, carnal octopi, and the Frida Kahlo of one troubled man's dreams, Carter's latest collection of creatures big and small is fascinating, unsettling and impossible to put down."

- Michael Landweber, author of *We* and *Thursday 1:17 p.m.*

"Carter is the best voice we have of the disconcerted male. These disquieting stories stay with you, tucked away in the odd-angled corners of your memory."

- Jeremy Trylch, author of *The Last Resort*

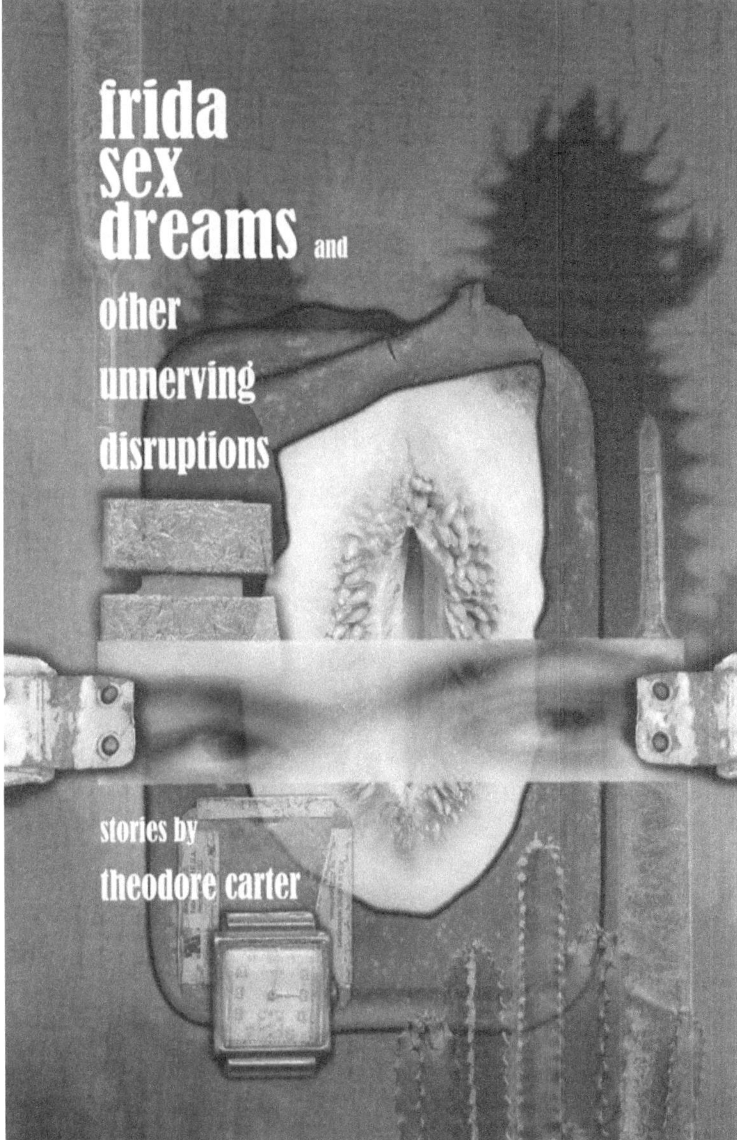

frida
sex
dreams and
other
unnerving
disruptions
stories by
theodore carter

Cover design by Courtney Granner

Author photo by Elizabeth Carter

ISBN: 978-1-7327097-1-3
Run Amok Books, 2019
First Edition

RunAmok

Printed in the U.S.A.

Contents

For Benjamin

Ena the Fairy's Eighteen and Over Show

Ena peeked around the red curtain, her wings tucked behind her back, and calculated the night's box office take in her head as she watched the audience file in. A vanilla-scented candle flickered on stage, Edward's idea, to create ambiance and mask the smell of sweat and mildew absorbed by the tent fabric during its summer-long journey through second-rate cities. The Victrola perched on the side of the stage played organ music, and the smell of popcorn and cotton candy wafted in like fog. Impatient patrons stood shoulder to shoulder chattering in a low murmur. Edward walked over and stood behind Ena.

She felt him there, turned toward him, and said, "We should start. We need to get four shows in tonight." He took out his snuffbox and inhaled the powder in it. His eyes grew wide and alert. Medicine for his toothache, he'd said, prescribed by a Baltimore dentist. He took it more often now than at the start of the summer. He talked about money a lot.

"Let 'em wait a bit. It makes them appreciate you," he said and hooked a finger inside the dirt-yellow ring of his white collar.

Outside the tent, fifty yards down the midway, the hand-painted "Ena the Fairy" sign depicted her in a sheer negligee with impossibly large breasts, her wings outstretched, glowing gloriously in rich titanium white. "Eighteen and over ONLY!," the sign read for no other reason than it increased desire for tickets. Ena wouldn't be 18 for another six weeks and couldn't remember the last time she'd seen anyone her own age. Edward didn't allow her out for fear of "giving away a free look."

Ena had watched a roadie paint the sign two days after her parents had sold her to Mr. Ivanov, the owner of the circus. Only 11 years-old and flat-chested, she'd felt thrilled and terrified when transformed by brushwork from an unwanted three-and-a-half-foot-tall winged abomination to a beautiful, mystical woman. Now, the plywood billboard's corners had chipped, and Ena could see spots where the roadies had touched

"""

up the faded color.

Edward sat down on a milk crate, put his hand on her shoulder, and turned her around so he could look her in the eyes. "You still get nervous. After all this time. I can tell."

"You're good with crowds," she said. "A natural."

He pulled at the ends of his waxed mustache bringing it to two fine points which he claimed detracted attention from his crooked teeth. "I am good. But you're good too. The difference is you hate it."

"You mix truth with lies," she said. "It's confusing."

He winked, his rouged cheek lifting up to his eye shadow. He kissed her on top of the head. Once Ena turned eighteen, Edward had said, he'd kiss her on the lips. Lately, he leered unapologetically, his eyes lingering on her breasts and legs as she dressed for the show.

He sprung to his feet and stepped through the curtain onto the stage. "Ladies and gentlemen, boys and girls . . ." He paused and peered out over the audience, pulled on his red suspenders, and contorted his face into a look of deep consternation. "That was a test. This is an eighteen and over crowd, correct? Because what you're going to see tonight, you may find disturbing, confounding, titillating. Arrouuuusing . . ." he rolled his eyes, then refocused, "Amazing. And even astonishing."

He went on like this for several minutes, a schtick he claimed created anticipation, shortened Ena's performance time, and established him as a roadblock, an annoyance, thus increasing the audience's sympathies toward Ena.

He gave his close-lipped smile, shook a tambourine to cue her entrance, and when she emerged through the parted curtain, Edward slapped the instrument creating a dramatic crash. She wore a white satin dress with lace overlay and a matching shrug, both custom-made for her in Boston at the start of the summer. Edward washed and mended the outfit between cities.

Her appearance silenced the crowd, and for several minutes, she walked back and forth on stage, hand on hip, a sultry turn at each end while Edward rambled on about her obvious authenticity. He said it took a full two minutes for the audience to take in what they saw, then several more minutes to convince themselves it must be a ruse. For this reason, Edward had her saunter from one side of the stage to the other for five minutes. "That way," he liked to say, "we can prove your marvelousness all over again."

"Some of you may doubt the authenticity of this angel from above," Edward said, which was Ena's cue to walk up the stairs onto the white, faux-marble podium at center stage and turn her back to the audience. Then, she extended her wings. Edward continued talking from the side of the stage, tracing the arc of her white-feathered wings with his outstretched hand. He walked over, unbuttoned her lace shrug, and removed it. The spaghetti straps underneath accentuated her lean shoulders. Her dress cut low in back to show feathered wings emerging from porcelain skin.

✳✳✳

The dress hugged her slender hips, then piled loosely at the base of the podium. When he unpinned her hair, it fell over her shoulders, down to the base of her wings, its jet black color a striking contrast to her pale skin and white feathers.

According to Edward, at this moment her beauty became so overwhelming, even to him who had seen her perform many times, that there was no need for speaking, music, or anything for almost thirty seconds. This, he admitted, was fifteen seconds too long, which created an unease in the audience he liked. It created twenty nine seconds of unease for Ena, to which Edward had said, "But darling, you become the perfect embodiment of virginal female beauty, more than perfect because there is a part of you that is inhuman."

"Are you saying I'm less than human?" she'd asked. Ena still carried the nasty things her mother used to say to her.

"I'm saying you are much greater," he'd said. "And, when you want to make real money, you can show more than your bare shoulders." He winked so that he could dismiss it as a joke, but Ena knew many female performers made good money entertaining customers after hours.

She fantasized about running away. She wanted to see towns and cars and shops, but feared regular folk, especially men, whom Edward had told her all desired her and would do almost anything to be with her. Another possibility was that on her eighteenth birthday, Edward would kiss her on the lips instead of the forehead, and they'd begin a grand romance financed by the box office money he stored in a cigar box. This fantasy felt closer and easier.

She stood tall on the podium, her back to the audience so that her face did not betray her wavering confidence. Her long black hair accentuated the elegant lines of her small body. Ena counted slowly to thirty at which point she turned around and smiled.

"There are among you skeptics who doubt the authenticity of this demure angel . . ."

Edward went on like this for several minutes while Ena extended her wings to their full span, pulled them in again, then out. The candle on stage flickered as Ena's wings sent a gentle breeze over the cramped audience. Her feathers brushed the tops of heads in the front row.

The climax of the show came when Edward said, "For those who remain skeptical, Ena would you please, if you will, be so kind, so accommodating, demonstrate your grace and beauty elevated to its highest degree by elevating into the air?"

Ena flapped her wings and ascended twenty feet to the apex of the tent. Then, she floated down in a slow glide, her legs and wings extended, hands at her side, hair fluttering like kite ribbons, back arched, a slight lean into the center pole, spiraling in her descent. She closed her eyes and everything slowed. The air felt good on her face and the train of the silk dress caressed her calves. She opened her eyes, glided onto the stage, and looked at the wide-eyed expressions in the crowd. At this moment, a split second before the cheering crescendo, she loved her audience. The applause came: loud, unapologetic, and simple. She bowed, smiled, waved, and rushed behind the curtain leaving Edward to wrap up. Truncating her appearances created repeat customers.

After four shows, she and Edward went back to their trailer. She tucked her wings in close to her shoulder blades and passed through the doorway of her cage, the same size cage used for the big cats in the menagerie. Once inside, she turned and saw Edward's closed-lipped smile beyond the bars. His lips curled up to match the curve of his handlebar mustache. Even with her, he hid his crooked, blackened teeth. He unbuttoned his yellowed collar and it fell away from his red-striped showman's shirt. "I hate doing this each night," he said, then latched and locked her cage door.

"I know," she said, "but you have to."

When she was twelve, a drunken sailor had taken her from her bed in the night. The roadies had grabbed their guns and found her in town at a bar tied to a chair amidst a crowd of heavy-drinking seamen. After that, Mr. Ivanov had hired Edward to take care of her and paid him with half Ena's box office take. Edward had brought the cage from the menagerie. "Now no one will ever take you away," he had said, and at the time, it sounded like a promise rather than a threat.

Now, as he looked at her through the bars, he said, "You're beautiful and smart. You should not be caged."

"I am small, desired, and valuable," she said.

She sat in the miniature bed Edward had built out of two-by-fours and down pillows. He'd covered the wooden exterior in purple velvet and lined the seams with rhinestones. He'd used broomsticks to construct a four poster bed and had draped mosquito netting over it. The contraption reached to the top of the cage.

"It's a paradox," he said.

"Don't think on it too hard," she said.

"I love you," he said.

"I love you too."

"It must be stifling," he said.

"What?"

"All of it." He gestured toward the interior of their cramped trailer. Costumes spilled out of the cardboard box in the corner. His shoe polish kit sat on the coffee table. An empty paper popcorn cone and a flyer for a local dental office lay on the floor. Edward took out his snuffbox, turned away from her, hunched over, and inhaled.

"The pain must be getting worse," she said.

"I need to get to Florida."

"Maybe you should go to a dentist before then, in the next good city. We must have money saved."

"Can't be laid up. Got to finish out the season."

Some of the other circus freaks had told her she should cut Edward loose, that she could do better on her own, that she should tell Mr. Ivanov. "I've seen this before," Helen the Bearded Lady had said as they sat across from one another at a picnic table with lunch plates of beans and cornbread. "He's probably an old pimp. That's where Ivanov found him." Ena didn't know whether or not Helen had been exaggerating or whether she really believed this. Before she could say more, Edward had come to the table and greeted them with a closed-mouth smile. Helen had looked down at her plate and continued eating.

Edward had said after the season ended, he'd line everything up, maybe get them a stage act in New York or something in Hollywood, but he needed money for clothes, travel, and to fix his teeth.

"You are everything to me, Ena," he'd said, his eyes wet and heavy.

In Greenville, South Carolina, after their final show, Edward sat her down, left the trailer, reentered holding a cake aglow with eighteen candles and singing "Happy Birthday." He placed the cake on the low table in front of her. She smiled so hard she could barely purse her lips to blow out the candles. Edward sat down in a winged chair. She looked up at him. His eyes met hers. He smiled, and she pulled her lace shrug over her low-cut dress. Ena blew out the candles.

"What did you wish for?" he asked.

After years of waiting for this day, she'd forgotten to wish. She looked up at him.

He chuckled. "It's okay," he said, and touched her arm. Goose bumps shot up.

He cut a thick slice of cake, put it on a plate, and handed it to her. He served himself, then leaned back in his chair to eat.

"It's great, Edward," she said.

"I remembered how much you liked those canned apples with cinnamon in Virginia, so I got Cook to make it with vanilla frosting and apples on the inside."

"It's perfect," She savored each forkful and imagined what the inside of a bakery full of such things might smell like.

They ate. Afterward, she hugged him, then he lifted her onto his lap and she folded herself up, her wings tucked in tight against her back, her head against his chest so that she could listen to the steady beat of his heart. Edward held her and stroked her hair. She waited for him to kiss her on the lips, to show her everything had changed. At the same time, she half-hoped he'd forget. Sex scared her. She didn't know if her body could withstand it, and she lay there afraid to move. He stroked her calf, then pushed the hem of her dress up and caressed her thigh. "You've been waiting for this day, haven't you?"

"Mmmm," she said.

"You're not a girl anymore, right?" he said moving his hand higher.

With his other hand, he ran his fingertips along the line of her neck and down her arm.

"Right," she said.

"I've been waiting for it too," he said, his hand moving up to the seam of her underwear.

When he kissed her, his stiff waxed mustache pressed against her lip. His tongue tasted sour in her mouth. He moved it around, and she copied the motion. She feared sex would hurt, that it might even be impossible given her size. He fondled her breasts over the satin dress. He unbuttoned her shrug and removed it as he'd done so many times on stage, then hooked a finger under the spaghetti strap and slid the dress off her shoulder leaving her bare to the waist. He traced her areola with his finger tips. He stroked and squeezed. She closed her eyes and tried to be the mythical, powerful, sexual Ena the Fairy of the midway billboard.

He brought her to his bed, lay her down on her back, took off his own clothes, and straddled her. Edward pressed his body onto hers and kissed her, his breathing heavy and loud. She embraced him and felt his ribs, his thin back. He pressed his genitals against hers. Her face was even with his black chest hair, and he smelled like pomade and sweat. He moved his hips, grinding into her, and he curled his back like a feeding beast as he kissed her. She spread her legs open to hasten the inevitable, and he tried to enter her but couldn't. For a moment, she feared this physical incompatibility would ruin everything, that Edward would want nothing to do with her. She'd be alone. He poked her again, this time making more headway. Ena did her best to spread wider, to open for him, and thought to herself *please God, let this work. Give me this piece of normal.* He entered her, and as she expected, it hurt. He began to move, slowly, to thrust in and out. She imagined the pain would dissipate, but it didn't. She only got used to it and realized it wouldn't get any worse, that there was nothing more to expect or fear. This pain, she decided, was something she could endure if she had to. This pain felt about right.

Edward closed his eyes. Ena closed hers too and hummed in a rhythm that matched his breathing and the pumping of his hips. She didn't know how much longer it would last and did her best to give to the push and pull of his body, to absorb his thrusts.

He reached his final triumphant exhale, a climactic grunt. She watched his clenched eyes open. He started to smile, then stopped himself, dismounted, and pulled on the ends of his mustache. His semen oozed out of her and ran down to her anus. She wanted to jump up and inspect it, to see if she was okay, to see how much of it was blood red. Instead, she smiled back at him. This was something she'd have to learn, not just for Edward, but for the next man too. When she sat up, she saw blood on the sheets. She'd heard this happened, but wondered if she bled more than other women because of her size, because her body wasn't actually capable of sex, wasn't enough for him. She wiped herself off with a towel, and they lay in bed together, her head on his bony chest, his arm hooked around her shoulders. He stared at the ceiling of the trailer, his mustache sad and limp.

"Happy Birthday, darling," he said.

She curled her legs up and moved deeper into the crook of his arm. She cried some, but did it quietly and so that it didn't change her breathing. He didn't notice.

They moved further south city by city, and while he packed and unpacked her small bed at each stop, she slept in Edward's bed at night. She would lay on her back, and he would kiss her, touch her, until she opened her legs for him and he entered her. The familiarity of sex made it increasingly endurable, though it did not become enjoyable. The pain continued. She'd lay on her back, eyes closed, and let her body absorb each thrust in an ebb and flow rhythm until he finished. What if she became pregnant? She imagined growing a winged abomination, something gnarled and wicked that might kill her as she birthed it. She still left spots of blood on the sheets, and she imagined she had a tear or cut that Edward reopened nightly. After sex, she slept burrowed into his body, feeling the lift and fall of his chest, inhaling the smell of his skin. Each morning, when Edward left the trailer, Ena would remove the sheets and clean them as best she could with a scrub brush. He pretended not to notice.

One day at lunch, Ena saw Helen alone at a table and Ena went to sit with her. "How ya doin'?" asked Helen.

Ena exhaled, then said, "Okay, but tired. Edward is insatiable. Had me up all night."

To which Helen lifted an eyebrow. She looked at Ena and chewed slowly. "Oh yeah?"

"Yes. Every night he wants it. It's tiresome, and," Ena whispered "a little painful." Ena watched Helen wanting advice but also hoping to shock her.

"How old are you, honey?" Helen asked.

"Eighteen."

Helen exhaled. "Old enough for some things, but not for others. Make sure he puts something on that toothpick before you two have it off."

Ena looked at her trying to figure out exactly what she'd said. Helen put down her fork, exhaled, and said, "I'll talk to Edward."

That night, before climbing on top of her, Edward unwrapped a small, queer package, then rolled a condom over his penis, and while Edward pumped in and out, Ena thought maybe Helen had saved her life.

They set up for a Wednesday opening in Macon, Georgia. To get people to come out, Mr. Ivanov priced beer half off. Ena's drunk crowd didn't pause at the right moments. A rowdy gap-toothed man in back yelled out answers to Edward's rhetorical questions. Edward steered the crowd as best he could. A man in the front row hooted and made cat calls during most of the show, cup in hand, a line of beer foam on his unkempt beard. When Ena made her flight from the top of the tent, the man reached up and grabbed hold of her ankle. She flapped her wings hard, feathers falling everywhere, before she shook loose of his grip.

"I almost fucking got her!" the man said, and laughed loud and long. Ena, safely back on stage, composed herself, smiled, and bowed. "Let's hear it folks for the Ena the Fairy, modern marvel, beautiful wonder. We hope you enjoyed the show,"

Edward took Ena's hand and led her backstage. Once there, he kneeled down and looked at her eye-to-eye. "Honey, I'm so sorry. Are you okay?"

She cried hard. Her body shook, and she burrowed into his chest. Her nose ran onto his striped shirt.

"It's okay. We'll get to Florida soon," he said.

He didn't touch her that night. She fell asleep with her head on his chest, but awoke to the rattle of overhead lights being ripped to the ground. The bearded man's voice, more slurred than before, yet distinct, called out "Where the fuck is she? Where's the fucking fairy? Hey fairy, where the fuck are you?"

Edward popped up and rushed out of the trailer in his underwear. Ena heard him say, "Look, you're going to have to leave."

She heard other voices join Edward: Nicky the sword swallower, Red, the curator of the skeleton museum, and the rants from the drunken man became more sporadic and distant.

Edward came back in, exhaled deeply, and said, "I can't imagine what it feels like for you."

"I feel safe with you. You're everything."

"You think I am."

"That's enough," she said.

"I hate to say it, Ena, but tonight . . ." he glanced over at the cage. She nodded, and she walked in and sat on her velvet-lined bed.

"Good night, Edward," she said.

He answered softly, "Good night."

✳✳✳

They made it down to Columbus, Alabama by late August and Mr. Ivanov planned to continue for a few more weekends before breaking for the season in Gibsonton, Florida. Edward said the southernmost swing would be a mix of hard-drinking good-ol'-boys and pious church going types, only the church going types weren't going to see Ena's eighteen and over show.

Edward went to his snuffbox often. He counted the crowd each night and talked about the box office percentage. At night, she went into her cage and when Edward turned out the lights, she stayed awake listening to the crickets and the sound of his breathing.

After the show in Albany, Georgia, Edward stood by his dresser counting the night's take.

"Edward," she said. "How much is in the cigar box?"

"Not enough," he answered as he slid off his bow tie.

"How much?"

"Why?"

"Just curious," she said.

He finished counting out the bills. He looked at her. She pretended to study her hands, but she watched as he put the money in his dresser drawer.

With only four stops left, they slid deep into the bowels of the cotton belt and the summer grew hot and humid. In Gainesville, before the show, Edward lit the vanilla candle on stage. Ena looked up at the tent's center pole, stretched her wings, and envisioned her flight pattern. She looked at Edward and noticed his candy striped shirt looked threadbare and yellowed while her dress looked as beautiful as the day Edward had bought it.

"We could use a big take tonight." He took a hit from his snuffbox. His eyes darted around as he surveyed the tent.

"I know," she said. "We've only got a few shows left." The end of the season and all of the promises wrapped up with it seemed further away the closer they got.

Fifteen people entered the tent for the first show, and Edward cursed under his breath behind the curtain. "That's it? Really? Goddamn this backwater city. Why'd we stop here?" He waited longer hoping for late arrivals, but no one else came. He bent down, looked Ena in the eye, and said, "You are Ena the Fairy. No matter how many people are here, you're a gorgeous anomaly of nature, and these folks are privileged to see you perform. You will wow them and word will spread. We'll end up on TV."

She nodded knowing he meant it. He pulled at the ends of his mustache then burst on stage. "Ladies and gentlemen, boys and girls . . ." He delivered his spiel as flawlessly as ever. Only

Ena noticed what had changed since May, how beads of sweat gathered on his forehead, how the bags under his eyes showed through the make-up, how sometimes he forgot himself and let his blackened teeth show when he smiled.

Ena wasn't sure what was supposed to happen in Gibsonton. All summer the idea had been abstract, beautiful, and far away. Now she knew there was nothing there. No Hollywood deal, dental surgery, or new suits, just the promise of another carnival season once winter thawed.

Ena hit her cues. The fifteen member audience ogled at her wings. They moved toward the end of the show, the routine so familiar she knew all of Edward's unwritten lines. "For those who remain skeptical, Ena would you please, if you will, be so kind, so accommodating, demonstrate your grace and beauty elevated to its highest degree by elevating into the air?"

Ena turned and locked eyes with Edward. She hooked her finger under the spaghetti strap of her dress and slid it off her shoulder. She did the same on the other side, and the dress pooled at her feet. She wore nothing underneath. Edward's mouth opened in surprise, then quickly closed to cover his teeth. The men hooted and whistled. Heart racing, Ena flapped her wings and ascended to the top of the tent. Amidst the shouts of male voices, she closed her eyes, arched her back, and glided down. Hot air passed over her bare skin, over her feathered wings. Her hair swirled behind her. She imagined she wasn't in the tent any longer, but outside in the night air flying hundreds of feet up over the carnival, amongst the stars, away from Edward, away from the summer, away from Florida. She was the Ena the Fairy from the midway billboard: bold, beautiful, sacrosanct.

She opened her eyes, and the dream was broken. She landed on stage and faced the audience with her wings outstretched, her naked body on display. The men clapped, whistled, and threw coins and bills onto the stage. She grabbed her dress from the podium, ducked behind the curtain, and covered up.

The din died down as the audience left. Edward came back

stage. Tears streaked his rouged cheeks, and he held a heap of crumpled bills.

"Ena," he said, "what happened?"

She shrugged, motioned with her hand at the money in his hands, and buried her face into his belly until her tears soaked his thin shirt. She inhaled his familiar scent.

That evening, they lay in bed together and he began kissing her as had become routine, but instead of waiting for him to climb on top of her, she nudged him onto his back, pulled his pants off, removed her dress, put a condom on him, straddled him, and rode him. She kept her eyes open and looked down on his contorted face, his eyes closed tight as he breathed heavily. He gritted his teeth in a careless way that allowed her to see their crooked edges. He moved his hips ineffectively, and she controlled the rhythm of sex, the in and out, the pain of it. For the first time, as Edward squirmed underneath her, as she watched him tilt his head back so far that she could see the tendons in his neck, Ena liked sex. She extended her wings out, her arms too, and flapped both together. The loose papers on the table ruffled in the breeze she'd created.

"Oh, Ena," he said, and she hoped he didn't speak again because it made it hard for her focus on her own body, the sensations of the pain, the cool air caressing her wingtips and her nipples. He strained and grunted as he came, but she did not stop, did not get off him until his penis went soft and limp.

She flapped her wings and rose up to dismount. Standing next to the bed, she looked at his naked body laid out over the sheets, his shriveled penis inside the messy, deflated condom. She put her dress back on, walked to his dresser, found the cigar box, took it out, and opened it. There wasn't as much money as there should have been. She took half of the bills and put them in Edward's dresser. She held onto the cigar box with the other half of the money."What are you doing?" he called from behind her.

She turned and saw him sitting up on the bed, the used condom in his hand.

"I'm leaving you," she said.

"You can't," he said. "We have a deal, and Mr. Ivanov hired me to protect you."

He went on talking, but she stopped listening. She took the box of condoms on Edward's dresser and placed it in the cigar box along with half the money. She walked outside. The moon was full and made the sky look like dawn. She extended her wings and took flight. Below her, Edward yelled something incomprehensible. She flapped hard and flew higher than she ever had before. Holding tight to the cigar box, she looked back over her shoulder. Her titanium white feathers glowed in the moonlight, and behind her, she could see the circles of the canvas tents. As she rose higher, the circus looked small and insignificant. The air smelled fresh and clear, free from the scent of popcorn, sugar, and Edward's pomade. She would never be the Ena the Fairy of the midway billboard. She would also never again be that scared 11-year-old girl waiting to see what would happen next.

Ginny looked carefully at Leopold's abnormally large paws as he slept perched atop the back of the couch. Now nearly six months old, Leopold should have been taking on the proportions of an adult cat. But, as his legs grew longer, they grew thicker. His nose protruded too much, and his ears were too wide. Still, according to her book, some kittens took longer to grow into their bodies, and looking at him—his narrowed eyes, his belly moving in-and-out with each breath—she felt guilty for questioning his appearance. She got up and stroked his back before walking toward the kitchen. Leopold opened his eyes, turned to look at her, and returned to his previous position.

She sat at the kitchen table with a cup of tea, and looked at the stack of envelopes in front of her. Bills mostly. She hated seeing them there each day, but couldn't bring herself to do anything about them either. Stan had taken care of the bills before. It wasn't that she couldn't figure out the finances herself. Every so often, she paid bills, though not monthly. In her mind, it was still Stan's job, and she resented the monthly reminders of Stan's passing.

She sifted through the stack of envelopes and read the return addresses. The sound of Leopold's rhythmic, guttural snores came in from the living room. She'd never imagined such sounds could be so comforting. "Get a pet," her friend Annie had said, and she'd scoffed, like getting a stupid animal could replace Stan. Eventually, Ginny followed Annie's advice. While most of her widowed friends had children about, were it not for Leopold, Ginny would be utterly alone. He did make things easier. Reflecting on this helped Ginny get out her checkbook, stamps, and a pen.

Two months later, she'd accumulated a new pile of bills. Ginny made a conscious effort to ignore them as she walked into the living room. Leopold paced next to the sliding glass window begging to go outside.

"What do you see out there, Leopold?" she asked.

He growled softly from deep in his throat. Ginny looked out the window and saw a squirrel with a spotted tail scamper up the oak tree.

Leopold's voice had grown deeper of late. Not meows, but growls. Almost deep roars. She no longer expected him to take on normal proportions. His high-arched shoulders had become more prominent, his canine teeth more pronounced, and he'd grown taller and more muscular.

"You want to chase the squirrel, Leopold?"

She slid the door open, and Leopold bolted onto the back lawn in just a few short strides. He leapt up against the tree trunk and pawed at the bark leaving long, deep scratches. (She'd had him de-clawed, but it didn't take.) The squirrel got away, but Leopold had gotten much closer than Ginny had expected. Leopold opened his mouth and roared, his white teeth gleaming. He paced around the tree making a guttural hum, his long tail twitching back and forth, his powerful shoulders moving with the rhythm of his gait. Ginny reached behind her and put her hand on the door handle so that she could get inside quickly if need be.

Two days later, Ginny found the same squirrel dead on the front stoop. She scooped it up with a dustpan, wrapped it securely in a plastic bag, then in another opaque paper bag. She didn't want anyone to know what Leopold had done.

Annie came over the next day for lunch. "Something's wrong, Ginny. He shouldn't look like that," said Annie.

Leopold started weaving between Ginny's legs affectionately. She reached down and scratched his head.

"He's a pound kitten, a peculiar mix of cat, that's all. Strange looking, but sweet."

Annie huffed. "You should take him to the vet, Ginny. He's getting too big. Too thick."

"Oh, he's beautiful," said Ginny picking him up. "Aren't you beautiful, Leopold?"

Leopold felt too heavy in her arms. He purred, and his rib

cage trembled like a lawnmower engine. Something was wrong, Ginny knew, but she wasn't going to take him to the vet so he could see how big Leopold had grown, how his claws had grown back. What if the vet wanted to take Leopold away?

Leopold started bringing more gifts to the front step. Jays, cardinals, and then crows. More squirrels, then raccoons, and once a fox about Leopold's same size. The carcasses were no longer intact either. Leopold tore hunks of meat from their bellies. Often, a bloody trail led down the front step. Ginny dutifully bagged each carcass and placed it deep inside her garbage can underneath her kitchen trash. Soon, Leopold brought these gifts so frequently that Ginny hardly had room in the can for her regular trash come garbage collection day.

"Leopold, you mustn't kill all of these animals," she said to him, but he only purred, and rubbed his head against her calf.

Annie called frequently, but Ginny put her off. She called one Saturday evening to see if Ginny was going to go to church.

"I've got too much to do tomorrow," Ginny said.

"Like what?"

"Bills, for one thing," Ginny said looking at the pile on the table.

"Bills?"

"Yes."

"By the way, have you taken that cat to the vet yet? Something's not right with him," Annie said.

"The vet says he's fine," she lied. "Just oversized."

In truth, Leopold was much larger than he'd been the last time Annie had seen him. Ginny tried to think back on how he'd looked when she'd picked him out at the pound, if he'd ever really looked like a house cat at all. Lately, she'd been looking through her old National Geographic magazines comparing him to the pictures of jungle cats. He bore a strong likeness to a jaguar in a 1978 issue.

"Something's wrong with him, Ginny. I'm telling you," said Annie.

"I've got to go now, Annie," said Ginny.

After that, Ginny stopped answering the phone. She rarely left the house. Leopold supplied all the companionship she needed. He'd grown so big that when he slept next to her in the bed, he made it sag just the way Stanley had. His snore sounded similar to Stan's too.

"Leopold, I don't know what I'd do without you," she said to him one night before turning out her bedside lamp. He narrowed his eyes, curled his lips, and licked his long, sharp teeth.

He had to be some sort of lion, jaguar, or puma. Whatever he was, she knew city ordinances would not permit his residency. Luckily, the fence around her yard was high enough to keep a secret. Most of Leopold's roaring occurred at night and could be explained away as squabbling raccoons if the need arose. People would find that more believable than the true explanation.

The more fearful she became of being found out, the more she grew to love Leopold. "I won't let anything happen to you," she told him as he laid his heavy head in her lap. She curled up with him on the couch letting her ear rest against his muscular belly. She listened to the strong thump of his heart, the heave of his lungs.

Every so often, the phone rang, or the doorbell, and Ginny ignored it. The sound of either made her straighten up in fear, as if someone was coming for the express purpose of taking Leopold.

She hated to do it, but Ginny restricted Leopold's time outdoors. She couldn't risk having him seen. A neighbor might call animal control. Plus, his killings had become problematic. The scrap meat she brought from the store wasn't enough. He started going after dogs. Some strays, but others with collars that Ginny would carefully remove from their dead bodies and hide in a shoe box. Once she caught Leopold laying in the backyard with some poor family's golden retriever ripped open in his forepaws.

"Leopold, you bad boy," she said. She walked closer to see

if she recognized the dog, but Leopold gave a menacing growl and pulled the carcass closer to his chest.

On the kitchen table, the bills piled up, and Ginny had less and less desire to do anything about them. Everything outside the house, outside of her and Leopold, seemed abstract. The phone never rang anymore, and Ginny presumed her friends had given up. Then, it occurred to her to pick the phone up and check for a dial tone. Nothing. She flipped through her stack of bills and found several "Final Notice" envelopes from the phone company. She threw them in the trash with satisfaction. She didn't want phone service anyway.

One morning, she woke up and flipped the switch on her bedside lamp. Nothing happened. She flipped the overhead light. Nothing. She quickly realized the electricity was out and thought of her unpaid bills. Leopold, awakened by her switch flipping, raised his head slowly and looked at her from his spot on the bed.

"What do we need it for anyway, Leopold?" she asked, and she came back to the bed and hugged him, placing her cheek against his so that she felt his wire-like whiskers.

"It's just us now, Leopold," she said.

But she hadn't thought it through. Nonpayment meant bill collectors. They started coming to the door almost daily. Some in company uniforms, others in suits, but each standing on the doorstep with papers, knocking loudly. Ginny peeked out on them from the bedroom window. So did Leopold, and they agreed not to open the door. "Can't they just leave us be, Leopold?" she asked him. No one could come inside where they might see Leopold.

Once, the brown-haired man in the tie began yelling through the door. "We'll have to foreclose." He said. The next day he yelled, "You have three days to remove your things, Mrs. Wells." He spoke in a deep, harsh tone and pounded on the door. Ginny knew to believe his threats.

Shutting herself in hadn't proved to be the glorious act of defiance she'd envisioned, and she wished to undo everything.

But at this point, she didn't know how much she owed and to whom. She'd thrown out the stack of envelopes. She could try to talk to these men, but that would mean opening the door and risk having them see Leopold. There was no use in having a home if Leopold wasn't in it. She could think of only one solution. The men had brought it upon themselves with their hounding.

For three days, she kept Leopold inside. She fed him sparingly, though it pained her to watch him stay hungry. He often stood in front of his feeding bowl whining. He pawed at the glass window and gave her his sad-eyed look. "I'm sorry Leopold. Soon, baby," she said to him. "You'll eat soon. You'll go out soon." Leopold paced through the house nervously. He roared at her. She could see the outline of his ribs through his fur.

When the brown-haired man in the tie knocked hard against the door, Ginny opened it. "Come into the living room," she said. As soon as he stepped in, Leopold jumped, hit him in the chest, and knocked him backward. Ginny slammed the door just in time to muffle his screams. She backed away quickly, and before the bill collector could get out another horrific shout, Leopold sliced his throat with his vicious claws.

Ginny retreated to her bedroom and let Leopold eat in privacy. She came back to the foyer hours later once Leopold had eaten his fill. She took the man's wallet from his torn pants and placed it in the shoebox along with the dog collars. Next, she sat down at the table with a glass of water. She looked at the spot where the bills had been and wondered how long it would be until Leopold got hungry again.

Ed peered through the morning fog and traced the path of the footprints along the beach. He kneeled down and placed his hand next to one. The footprint looked about eighteen inches long. Three clawed toes splayed out from the center. Between each toe, the sand lay flat and even, the faint impressions of webbing. When Ed conjured up a creature in his head that could have made the prints—something big, bipedal, clawed-toed, with webbed feet—he saw an enormous bird, like a semi-aquatic ostrich.

Ed stood up and looked for someone else to whom he could show the footprints. It was the Tuesday after Labor Day. The summer morning sounds of scampering, shell-gathering kids had been replaced by lonely seagull caws and the rhythmic rumble of waves. About a hundred yards in the distance, a man emerged from the fog. His head moved from side to side as though he were scanning the beach for something. The man approached. Ed thought he looked about his own age, mid sixties. The man's eyebrows were knit in worry, the wind blew his thinning hair, and he squinted behind his glasses.

"Excuse me. I'm looking for our dog. A black lab. Have you seen him?"

"No. Sorry," said Ed. The man turned and looked down the coastline. "Okay. Thanks anyway."

"He have a tag with a phone number?"

"Yeah."

"I'll call if I find him," said Ed. "I'm here a lot."

"Thanks," said the man. He turned to leave, and Ed said, "Hey, what do you make of these footprints?"

The man took a step toward them and looked down. "Yeah. I don't know."

"What do you think made them?" Ed asked.

The man shrugged. "Not much of a nature guy, to be honest."

The man walked off. The fog wrapped tight around Ed in

perfect incongruence with the vast expanse of the ocean, and the rising sun gave everything a soft, orange glow.

✳✳✳

Ed opened the door of the condo. Carolyn stood behind the kitchen counter in her bathrobe. Her shoulder-length brown hair stuck up on one side, and she held a package of coffee grounds.

"Hey, honey" she said without turning.

"Hey."

"You wipe all the sand off your feet?"

He looked down. Sand clung to the tops of his feet. "Yeah," he said, then stepped out into the hallway to brush off the sand.

He came in again and sat on a stool across the kitchen counter from her. "Carolyn, I saw something today. Huge footprints from some kind of bird."

She scooped coffee into the machine and stayed silent for a beat. Next, she manufactured a smile and leaned over the counter to kiss him. The scent of her skin mixed with the brewing coffee. He loved her for not saying more.

"They're unusual is all I'm saying, something I haven't seen before, and I just wonder what made them."

"What do you think made them?" He recognized her question as a test. She turned toward the refrigerator and got out some bread. He watched the elegant lines of her thin neck, unchanged in their decades together.

"Whatever made them had claws." As he told her about it, he became less certain of its spectacle. "Had to be something bigger than any bird I've seen out there."

She put four slices of bread in the toaster.

"Well, now what are you going to do?" she said.

"I don't know. I was thinking I'd go to the state park. Maybe try to talk to a ranger there."

"And tomorrow, you're going to be out on the beach an hour earlier?"

"Well, yeah. Taking my camera phone too"

"It'll be dark. You should wear a head lamp."

"Good idea," he said, though after he said it, he thought maybe she'd been teasing him.

"And maybe think about forming a search committee. Tell all the neighbors. Maybe notify the Cape Gazette?"

"It's interesting. That's all."

"I shouldn't tease. It's great. A puzzle to work on, and maybe you'll learn something."

"I know, just don't take it too far."

She smiled.

✳✳✳

Beams of light from Ed's headlamp and flashlight bounced along the path in front of him as he walked toward the beach. He'd brought a backpack this time filled with a water bottle, his camera phone, and plaster for making a cast. Posted to the boardwalk leading over the sand dunes, Ed saw a flyer picturing a lost black labrador named Jellyfish. He thought of the man he'd seen the day before.

The low tide left a wide swath of sand exposed. Ed walked slowly, his lights oscillating across the beach in search of footprints. As he made his way toward the cliffside, the ascending sun threw pink across the landscape. He knew this to be the kind scenery he should stop and appreciate, the kind Carolyn would point out, but he didn't have time for it.

An hour later, with the sun firmly in the sky, he found prints fifty yards up the beach from where he'd seen them the previous day. This time, with the tide at its lowest point and no fog, he could follow their path almost to the cliffside before they disappeared into the water. He took pictures with his phone from every conceivable angle. Placing his own foot next to the print, he compared scale. He zoomed out to give a sense of the creature's path and gait. Someone might be able to study the distances in between and make a determination about the creature's anatomy.

He took out the plaster and mixed it in a cup, but it poured out too heavy and crushed the sandy edges of the footprint. The plaster set, but the resulting cast made it look as if the creature walked with frying pans strapped to its feet. The claws came out beautifully which was enough to make Ed feel he'd salvaged some value from the mold.

As Ed made his way back home, the sun blazed an August-hot heat. A few walkers and a couple of middle-aged surfers began making their way out onto the beach. Ed saw a woman walking up and down the beach, stopping periodically to scan the expanse. "Piiiiiicklllllllllles!" Then, a pause, and "Here, Pickles" while she slapped her knee. Another lost dog.

✱✱✱

Later that morning, Carolyn sat next to Ed on the couch, and he handed her the plaster cast. She knit her brow and rotated the hard plaster first one way, then another.

"You see here? These are the toes. You can see the ball of the foot there."

"What's all this?" she asked, pointing to the blob-like mass near where the creature's heel should have been.

"Well, the sand is soft. It kinda lost its shape when I poured the plaster, but you can still see it, right?" He traced the outline where the imprint should have been.

He took out his phone and gave it to her. She slid through the pictures, tilted the phone and leaned in. "It is unusual," she said. "You think it's some bird?"

"They're too large for that," he said.

"What do you mean?"

"Plus, yesterday and today? I saw people out looking for lost dogs."

"You think this creature ate their dogs?"

It was a stretch, and while the thought had crossed his mind, he shouldn't have said it. "It's just unusual. These prints start showing up, and people are losing their dogs."

"Stay in bounds, Ed."

"I am. I just want to see it for myself, to know what's making the prints."

"That's sounds perfectly sane and logical. Almost like birding or wildlife photography."

"Exactly."

"Almost," she said, "only at four in the morning with headlamps, plaster casts, and dead dogs."

✹✹✹

He'd overslept and the sun bathed the beach in its soft morning glow. As he walked along the water's edge toward the distant rocks, he saw a mound of brown on the beach. At first, he thought it might be seaweed. As he came closer, he saw and heard flies swarming above the mass. Coming closer still, he smelled the sour stench of rot and saw pink entrails spilling out of matted fur. The flies dissipated upon his arrival, but returned and buzzed about him once he stopped moving. He found the face of the beast. Its white teeth, jagged and pronounced, emerged from receding gums. Large black eyes pushed outward from the animal's sockets. He traced the shape of its body and recognized the animal as a dog, though distorted in death, bloated in some places, scrawny and bent in others, its coat lackluster like a threadbare blanket. Three stripes of pink flesh showed along its ribs, a claw mark matching the footprints. Ed took pictures.

Back at home again, he sat next to Carolyn on the couch, showed the pictures, and pointed out the similarities between the claw marks and the footprints.

"This is disgusting." She pushed the phone back to him. "I think you should see somebody again."

"There's nothing wrong with me."

"You're misconstruing things, making them more fantastic than they are."

"The footprints are real. That dog is real."

"It's a dead dog. There's no magical beast to blame."

"I said unknown, not magical."

She stopped and exhaled. "Just talk to someone about it?"

"I'm talking to you."

She got up, put her hands behind her head, and walked toward the kitchen.

✳✳✳

Ed had planned to call the police and to be on the beach when someone — the police, animal control, sanitation — came to pick up the dog. He wanted to ask their opinion as to what happened. Was an enormous clawed bird on a killing spree along the Delaware coast? Maybe several clawed birds? Or, maybe Carolyn was right, and he'd convinced himself of magic where none existed.

Instead, he sat on the balcony with a cup of coffee and listened to the rumble of the waves, felt the salt-scented wind blow through his thinning hair. He wanted Carolyn to see him there, evidence of his indifference. He had a narrow view of the ocean between the two houses in front of his and watched the waves roll in. A copy of "Shipwrecks of the Delaware Coast," lay in his lap, but he couldn't focus long enough to get through a page.

Behind the screen door, he could hear Carolyn emptying the dishwasher in the kitchen. He hoped she'd come apologize or ask him if he wanted lunch, something. He would have apologized to her if he thought it would help. She'd put up with a lot over a long time, indulged him, coddled him, and took him to see a doctor when he'd gone too far. Promising to change would be empty. Instead, he waited, listened to her footsteps, to her opening and closing her drawers, to the clatter of the dishes.

That evening, she said to him, "I'm not mad, Ed. I'm just run down."

"I know," he said, "That's worse. I'm sorry."

She walked away. That night, he pretended to fall asleep on the couch while watching the Yankees. He couldn't be next to her in bed without trying to explain everything, and he knew she couldn't stand hearing him talk anymore. He lay there listening to the drone of the sportscasters and the sounds of

Carolyn getting ready for bed—the opening and closing of the bathroom door, the squeak of the mattress springs as she settled in.

He woke up at five without an alarm, sat up on the couch, and looked out the window at the gray sky. He thought it might impress Carolyn if she woke up to find he had not gone out to the beach, that he'd slept in. He spent ten minutes thinking about this, then ten more minutes getting dressed and hurrying down to the beach.

Soon after traversing the boardwalk with the poster of Jellyfish, he saw a trail of prints broken occasionally by the ebb and flow of the tide. He followed the tracks, losing them several times but always picking them up again further down the beach. They lead him to the cliffside, then disappeared into the water.

Ed peered into the nooks and crannies of the rocks out in the water hoping to see an unknown species of bird. He noticed a small cave accessible only through the water and waded into the ocean. The cold stung his toes. To get to the cave entrance, he'd have to swim. He got a plastic sandwich bag out of his backpack and put his cell phone in it. Then, he swam, bag and all, to the small opening.

Still in the water, he entered the cave and turned on his headlamp. The pool opened up to a vast underground expanse. He wondered if anyone knew about this, if the historical society had mapped it. Maybe his eyes were the first human eyes to see this.

The waves pushed him gently back and forth as he peered into the cave. Light from his headlamp penetrated the deep recesses, yet he couldn't see the cave's end. He traced the edge of the water to a small sand embankment where he found dozens of the mysterious footprints in the sand. This was the creature's home. The beast only came out early in the morning with the low tide. The rest of the day, water covered the mouth of the cave.

A large wave crashed against the cave's entrance. Just as Ed turned toward the noise, water shot through the narrow opening like a cannon ball and knocked him down. He hit his face against a rock. Laying on his belly, he put his hand to his face and felt the warm blood. He splashed water on his cheek to clean the wound. The salt stung.

His face ached and throbbed with his heartbeat. He got out his phone, and turned on the camera function so that he could see his face. When he did, the severity of his injury surprised him. The left side of his face dripped crimson. He took off his shirt and pressed it against his cheek.

Ed looked more closely at his surroundings. Based on the number of prints, the variety of their sizes, and their multitude of directionality, Ed estimated there to be several three-clawed creatures inhabiting the cave. He looked at the shapes of the rocks and boulders, around their edges, to see if an animal lay watching him, but he saw nothing.

Even with his headlamp, trying to make out the contours of the cave proved futile. Ed listened for the sound of movement. All he heard were waves beating against the side of the cliff, the water pouring into the cave entrance, then receding back out. He looked at the beach on which he sat and studied the criss-crossing footprint patterns.

His bleeding stopped. He removed the balled up, blood-stained shirt from his face. He looked at where he'd entered, but the tide had come up and that narrow entrance had almost disappeared. Ed needed to leave before he became trapped by the rising tide.

He stepped out into the pool of water, and a wave burst through the narrow passage like spray from a shotgun and knocked him backward. He attempted again, this time ducking under the water and trying to swim through, but again the push of the waves coming in forced him backward. With every failed attempt, time passed and the tide rose making escape more difficult. The rising water level ate away at the cave's beach too.

He realized he'd need to wait for low tide and returned to the embankment. Water had almost closed the cave mouth entirely and darkened the cave so that he could hardly see. He felt his way to a space between two rocks where he could sit protected in case whatever animals had made those footprints were to emerge from the darkness. He wanted to call Carolyn to let her know what'd happened, but his phone didn't get reception. He pulled his knees to his chest, listened, and waited for his wet clothes to dry. Nothing but the sound of the waves, the low bellow of the ocean crashing against the walls around him. Light waned to a mere shimmer coming off the water. Ed closed his eyes. Hours passed.

Then, he heard a sound like a low dog growl only higher in pitch. He opened his eyes and saw the silhouette of a creature looming above him. It stood nearly seven feet tall, broad shouldered with tufts of feathers sticking out at its sides and on top of its slender head. The beast's beak jutted out toward him like a weapon, its neck bobbing like that of a chicken. Ed flinched thinking that one of these movements would be a thrust toward his face like a snake striking. He remembered the dog carcass, the ripped flesh, and looked at the creature's feet. Three long claws jutted out from enormous webbed feet. The source of the footprints revealed.

The giant bird leaned toward him. It growled again, a guttural noise from its ostrich-like neck. The bird let out a loud squawk, and the sound reverberated against the cave walls.

He reached for his camera phone and pointed it at the bird. He'd have to use the flash. It'd likely scare the beast, and he knew what those claws could do to flesh. Still, he'd only be hastening an encounter that'd likely take place before low tide anyway. He needed that picture. Without it, the bird didn't exist. No matter what happened, someone would eventually find his body and his phone. Someone would show Carolyn, and when they did, he wanted her to have something to see, a valid reason for everything.

Ed imaged Carolyn looking with reverence at a picture of the creature's plume of red and blue feathers, the enormous crooked beak, the opalescent eyes, and scaly neck. If this bird existed, what else might be out there? The image would be an apology for everything. He'd gift Carolyn a glimpse at the impossible, and she would understand why he couldn't help hurting her over and over, why she had to find him dead in this cave. Their years together would be justified, worthwhile. Not "I told you so," but more of a "I just couldn't help it, and now you know why."

He pressed the button on his camera phone. The flash lit up the creature's head and bounced off the cave walls. The bird lifted one leg high in the air near Ed's face giving him a clear look at the sharp claws which had so clearly marked the dog's carcass. The creature's eyes grew beautifully wide and angry, and it let out a deafening, blood-curdling shriek.

The Thirty-Ninth President and the Fourteenth Tentacle

"It was big, it was very bright, it changed colors and it was about the size of the Moon. We watched it for ten minutes, but none of us could figure out what it was. One thing's for sure, I'll never make fun of people who say they've seen unidentified objects in the sky."

— President Jimmy Carter, 1969

1969

Xenia sat in the copilot's seat and wore one more stripe on her armband than Veltra, a distinction Xenia feared had become meaningless. By now, Veltra knew Xenia loved her, and she'd become increasingly insubordinate.

"Don't scare them, but make sure we're seen," said Xenia.

Veltra scowled. "I know the routine." She steered the craft in a big looping figure eight and flicked on the illumination switch. Through the vessel's viewports, Xenia could see the ship's garish, pulsating lights.

Veltra left the craft in hover. She removed her flight helmet and let her tentacles hang haphazardly around her face, over her beautiful eye. "I can't believe we're doing this," Veltra said.

"We follow orders," Xenia said. She straightened her own helmet and reached underneath to make sure the rubber band held her tentacles in place in accordance with protocol.

"We're the top pilots they've got, and we're here harassing a peanut farmer?"

"We wouldn't have been asked if it weren't important."

"It's embarrassing," said Veltra.

Xenia peered through the scope at the crowd of humans and spotted their target: the well-groomed, sandy-haired man.

"Does he see us?" asked Veltra.

"Not sure."

"What's fuck's his problem?"

"We're not supposed to use that word. It offends them,

especially him. Turn on the engine sounds." Xenia spoke firmly in an attempt to convey authority.

Veltra pushed a button and faux engine noise started up. The craft thundered like a fossil fuel machine. She turned the dial up on the lights too, and the ship began to hum with the output of luminescence.

Still peering through the scope, Xenia said, "We may need to go lower."

"Fuck, fuck, fuck, fuck," said Veltra. "Why don't we just sit here until one of their clunky airplanes hits us with a cannonball."

"Wait. Wait. I think he sees us. Do something grand."

Veltra sent the ship into a dive so quickly that it pushed Xenia's back against her chair for a second before the g-force regulator activated. Then, she pulled the ship out of the dive, hovered, and sped off. "That do it?"

"Yeah," answered Xenia. "His eyes got nice and big."

1971

"I don't understand why we always get the peanut farmer. I mean, why not mix it up some? I'd like to see the other side of earth. Check out Brezhnev," said Veltra.

"Renia and Hexa are on him," said Xenia.

"They could at least assign us President Ford."

"The commander says we focus on this human."

"For how long?" asked Veltra.

They hovered above the Georgia Governor's mansion. "Looks pretty flat on top. I could just set the ship down right there. Maybe set it down hard and shake him out of bed."

Xenia looked at Veltra in profile, the straight vertical pitch of her face, the sheen of her perfect mucus covering. Months ago, before on an exploratory mission to Mars, she and Veltra had rubbed their fourteenth tentacles together until they both erupted in orgasm, then collapsed onto the ship's floor, exhausted and satiated. They never spoke of it. Now, the incident had become an unspoken secret that Xenia feared Veltra would use with their commanding officer if need arose.

"We're not to cause a panic."

"If you ask me, we're going about this all wrong, too slowly," said Veltra.

"No one's asking you. Follow orders," said Xenia.

They waited and listened to the crickets chirping in the night. Then, Veltra silently lowered the craft onto the roof. "Now what?"

"Wait," said Xenia.

Veltra exhaled dramatically, blowing a tentacle out her face as she did so.

"You know, you should wear your helmet during missions," said Xenia.

"I know it," said Veltra, but she didn't make a move to correct the problem.

Soon, several men in dark suits emerged from a rooftop doorway and ran toward the ship with guns in hand. Veltra ran to the external scope to get a close-up look at them.

"Is the peanut farmer among them?" asked Xenia.

"Nope," said Veltra.

"Let's use the freeze ray," said Veltra, and before Xenia could think about it, much less authorize it, Veltra pressed the button and the men froze in place. Veltra and Xenia exited onto the roof and walked by the armed men who stood like statues. "He's going to do that shocked, big-eyed thing humans do. He won't hear a word we're saying to him."

"It a process," said Xenia.

"Jesus," said Veltra.

"Jesus?" said Xenia.

"Some dead guy they like to invoke."

"I don't think you're using that right," said Xenia.

"Oh, I think I am," said Veltra.

They found Jimmy Carter standing in the hallway, hunched, against the wall, his skinny legs sticking out of a baby blue bathrobe. He held a brass candlestick in his hand and as they approached, he raised it high as if about to strike. Veltra had been right. His blue eyes were opened wide, and his lower lip trembled.

Xenia spoke. "Jimmy, we're not going to hurt you. We think you should run for president."

Jimmy's white-knuckled grip on the candlestick loosened and he lowered it just a bit. "President? Really?"

"You'll see us again," said Veltra. "And again. Take a good look now so you won't be surprised."

Jimmy stood up from his cowering position, leaned forward, and squinted. Then, slowly, he reached out his free hand toward Veltra. "I wouldn't do that," said Veltra. "Our mucus layer is toxic to humans," she said, which wasn't true.

"Speaking of toxic, we've got some problems on our home planet . . ." said Veltra.

"Not now!" said Xenia, and she pulled her copilot back down the hallway.

"Why are you here?" Jimmy yelled after them.

Xenia stopped, turned and said, "We want you to tell people we exist. Gradually. Get them used to the idea."

1976

"He's not stupid. He's probably figured it out already," said Xenia

"That rube? He doesn't know which end is up," said Veltra. "He's in over his head."

"When beings from another planet come to talk, obviously they want resources or to set up trade."

"Is that what he looked like he was ready to do when we first met? Looked like he wanted to give you a candlestick in the neuron cavity."

"That was years ago," said Xenia. "Our relationship has grown."

"*Human* years. Like those mean anything."

"We're here to complete our mission, not question it," said Xenia.

"I know, sweetie," said Veltra. "I'm sorry." But Xenia knew she didn't care. Veltra slid her twelve tentacle around Xenia's midsection, obviously trying to warm up to the fourteenth. Xenia let her for a minute, then she looked into her gray eye and saw her poisonous lust. She wanted to succumb to it, embrace it, but mustered the fortitude to say, "Stop, Veltra. This is not the place. Besides, I'm your commanding officer."

"No one's looking," said Veltra, a sultry look pouring out of her optical nerve. Xenia hated Veltra's beauty which churned up hideous jealousy and temptation. Still, Veltra was right. No one was looking. They'd gotten so little direction on this mission, Xenia had begun to wonder about its importance.

"I'm going to see Jimmy," said Xenia. Without waiting for Veltra to respond, Xenia teleported down to the Plains, Georgia campaign headquarters in the converted train depot.

Jimmy was alone, head in his hand, leaning over papers at a desk. Xenia swished her tentacles making a squishing noise that caused him to turn and see her.

"Hi, Xenia," he said. He looked older, worn, and had bags under his eyes.

"How's the campaign going?"

"Pretty good, until recently. Darn Playboy Interview."

"Would it help if I exterminated someone on your behalf?"

"No, no," he said smiling. "I know you mean to help, but please don't make that offer anymore."

Xenia had come to accept that there were many things about Jimmy she would never fully grasp. Still, she liked being with him, appreciated his calm demeanor, thoughtful pauses, and easy smile. So different than talking with Veltra where every conversation felt like a power struggle and dripped with sex.

Xenia said, "Jimmy, you need to speed things up. We want to inhabit earth. Our planet is dying."

"I know, Xenia, but it's a careful balance. I talk about you when asked."

"In vague language."

"I'll lose the election if I do more. Then where would you be?"

Xenia didn't know the answer to that. She could only assume others were building a relationship with President Ford. "I suppose you'll have more leeway to speak when you're president."

"I hope so. Say, where's Veltra?"

"Truth is, Jimmy, we're having a hard time, she and I. I suspect she's been messing about when on leave, too." Xenia wasn't expecting to say it, but now that she had, it sounded definite.

"I'm sorry Xenia. We're all sinners. Best we can do is try to be decent from this day forward."

"Decency. That's a good trait," said Xenia.

"That's what I'm campaigning on," said Jimmy. Then he turned back to his papers, a clear sign the conversation had ended, and Xenia teleported back to the ship. Once there, she couldn't bear to look at Veltra.

1979

"They keep a close eye on that airspace. We'll have to teleport down to the White House," said Xenia.

"Why don't we just fly down anyway and vaporize the fossil fuel machines in our way?" asked Veltra.

Xenia shot her a look. "You know that'd compromise our mission."

Veltra disliked teleporting. The tractor beam dried out her mucus layer, and she took pride in her luscious sheen.

"Fine, I'll go then," said Xenia. She'd been doing a lot of the face-to-face work herself lately.

"Don't get your tentacles tangled, Xenia. I'll go."

They stood in the teleport chamber and let it zap them down into the oval office. Jimmy sat staring down at his desk looking haggard. Veltra made a humming noise she thought sounded like human throat clearing. Jimmy looked up.

"Oh, good afternoon," Jimmy said, putting on a strained smile. "Both of you this time. Veltra, I'm glad to see you haven't forgotten me."

"Of course not, Jimmy," said Veltra. "The thing is, it's been a long time since we first met, and you still haven't prepared your people for our arrival."

"It'll take time. I've got this hostage situation, an energy crisis, runaway inflation . . ."

"I'm growing weary of excuses, Jimmy. You promised things during your campaign."

"I'm working on it. Haven't I spoken out about UFOs more than any other president?"

"That is true," said Xenia.

"We aren't UFOs. We can be identified, need to be identified," said Veltra.

"Please be patient," said Jimmy.

In disgust, Veltra unfurled her long, thick tongue and licked the presidential seal on the office rug, the ultimate sign of disrespect. Jimmy looked confused.

"Please excuse her," said Xenia. She hugged Veltra and pressed the teleport button on her utility belt sending them back to the ship. Once there, Veltra touched her face, checking the moistness of her mucus layer.

Xenia said, "You're reckless."

"He's docile and weak. It's time for action."

"He's kind and honest."

"We're flying around in obscurity while our planet withers and dies."

"Be patient."

"I like this Ronald Reagan guy."

"He's just a movie cowboy."

"Better than a peanut farmer."

1981

"I'm leaving," said Veltra. She gathered a few sprigs of homegrown vegetation and some extra gear for her utility belt.

"Headquarters will not look kindly on your insubordinate behavior."

"Headquarters can lick my fourteenth tentacle, if they're even paying attention. This mission failed long ago. You just haven't noticed yet," said Veltra.

Xenia had no response for that. She too worried that their

lack of directives indicated headquarters' indifference. She'd heard two younger agents were working on Reagan, a couple more on Gorbachev.

Veltra stood in the teleport portal. She touched the mucus layer on her face which had become duller and drier over the years. "So long, Xenia."

"I will miss you, Veltra," she said.

"I know you will, but I was poison to you. I ate you up."

"But I'd grown accustomed to it and will miss it."

"We're both frightfully unhappy," said Veltra.

"It's the mission. It was flawed from the get," said Xenia

"Don't blame it on Jimmy. I am cruel and predatory," said Veltra. Xenia hadn't realized Veltra's level of self-awareness. "I can't help it. Goodbye," said Veltra, and she left.

✳✳✳

Xenia looked around the empty vessel. Already, Veltra's departure gave her relief. It also made her lonely. She moved toward the monitor near the pilot's seat and found an old message from headquarters, one that reminded her of why she'd come to earth in the first place. It said, "Jimmy Carter is known as trustworthy and kind. The people of the world will believe what he says about us. But, we must act fast. Humans are fickle." All of Xenia's experience confirmed this statement.

2003

Through the monitor, Xenia saw Jimmy sitting on a grass knoll looking pensively out over a pond. She got into the teleport chamber and went to him. He turned toward her.

"Oh, hello, Xenia. You know, it's unnerving how you arrive like that."

"Sorry," she said. "Everything okay?"

"No," he said. "There is suffering all over the world."

"Yes, and in other places too."

"I suppose." He picked up a rock and threw it into the water. "I did my best for you, but I just couldn't get there. I'm still the only president who has admitted to seeing . . ."

Xenia interrupted. "And, uh, Reagan too."

"Oh. Yes."

"Sorry to bring that up."

Xenia looked at Jimmy's profile. In it, she could see the young, sandy-haired optimist she'd known years before, though his face had become wrinkled, his hair white. The sun began to set behind them casting long shadows over the water.

"Am I still your mission?" Jimmy asked.

"In a sense," Xenia answered. She'd grown old too. Headquarters had since realigned priorities but had failed to reassign her. Deep down, she knew they'd forgotten her. They didn't even ask for a ship log anymore. Still, she followed Jimmy, pretending she thought it her duty.

"You ever hear from Veltra?" Jimmy asked.

"She's doing quite well. Confidant to the Supreme Commander." Xenia had heard she'd used her fourteenth tentacle to get there, but stayed there because of her ruthless guile.

"You miss her?" Jimmy asked.

"Yes, but I'm glad she's gone," said Xenia.

"I understand," said Jimmy, but how could he possibly, this honest man, husband, father, humanitarian, former Supreme Commander of Earth? Still, she appreciated his compassion for her, and for everyone.

The sun had set. Xenia moved closer to him. Without understanding why, she slowly slid her thirteenth tentacle onto his arm.

He turned quickly toward her. "Aren't you toxic to me?" he said.

"Veltra lied," she said.

He smiled uneasily. Xenia, overtaken by a perverse desire to see how far she could take things, tried the fourteenth tentacle, sliding it slowly up his arm and onto his shoulder. She rubbed it back and forth on his flannel shirt, her pleasure rising. Jimmy looked at her, a pasted on smile exposing large, yellowed teeth. Unaware, but clearly uncomfortable. Aroused by her own rash action, Xenia continued. She'd never done anything like this, anything so sinister, deceptive, aggressive, and selfish. Jimmy lifted his hand slowly, placed it on top of her fourteenth tentacle, and patted it. Xenia's tentacles tingled. A rush of warmth shot through each one of her extremities. She pushed her fourteenth tentacle into his hand and moved it back and forth more quickly until it pulsated, waxed and waned. Soon, she could no longer hold off the release of pleasure. Xenia climaxed and moaned. Jimmy looked at her quizzically, as if he might have an idea as to what happened, but Xenia didn't care. Exhausted, exhilarated, she let her tentacle fall from Jimmy's shoulder and exhaled deeply, half wanting him to know what she'd done, how badly she'd abused him.

He turned away and looked out over the pond. Part of her felt guilty for what she'd done. She knew it'd been wrong to take advantage of his naivety, but she also hated how easy it'd been. Everyone had taken so much from this great, kind man. But at the same time, in the back of her head, she heard Veltra's voice saying that Jimmy had done it to himself, really.

Xenia ran her fourteenth tentacle through the grass wiping off the excess mucus. "You know, this human rights thing, it could easily be extended to go beyond humans. You could do that for us. You owe me that much." He turned toward her and smiled again, a smile that showed how tired he'd become, how weak and ineffectual. It made Xenia feel foolish for being there. Light years away, her planet was dying, Veltra continued to wield and trade power, and younger agents embarked on relevant missions.

"I'm old, Xenia. I will die before too long."

"You never know, Jimmy," which she knew didn't make a lot of sense. She didn't know much about the human lifespan.

"I don't want to be remembered as the alien president."

"There are worse things," said Xenia.

"I will leave it in God's hands," said Jimmy. "And God's hands will receive me."

"Jimmy," said Xenia, "You don't even know if God has hands."

He laughed, but Xenia didn't think it funny. She looked out over the horizon at the fading sun lamenting her patience and affection for this flawed human and wished she were needed elsewhere.

Frida Sex Dreams

I fall asleep next to Melissa underneath our new Ikea bedspread, but soon I'm in a dream looking down at Frida Kahlo laying on her back in her four-post canopy bed, knees bent and legs open. She hikes up her long skirt exposing her pale thighs and peers at me from underneath her famous unibrow. I've seen the same challenging, unnerving stare peering out of the canvas in her self-portraits. Holding eye contact, she reaches a hand down and begins touching herself. "Te gusta?" she asks. She reads my discomfort, starts laughing, then rubs herself harder. A big hearty bellow erupts from the darkened corner of the room. I turn my head and see an immense Diego Rivera emerge from the shadows. He's wearing a large-brimmed hat and heavy miner shoes. He's giant, maybe seven-feet tall, and of prodigious girth. He's rocking back and forth from heel to toe. His laugh grows loud and he points at my crotch.

In defiance of my psychological discomfort, my penis swells to an enormous erection and throbs as if in possession of its own heartbeat. Soon, it's of cartoon-like proportions. I look like one of the fertility idols that made me and Melissa giggle on our trip to Thailand. It's painful. Frida's laugh morphs into a cackle. She's rubbing her clit in quick circles, and with her free hand, she points at my penis too. The din of Frida and Diego's laughter mutates into a unified screech. As the decibels increase, my penis swells until I fear it may burst, blood erupting from my shaft like some horrific ejaculation.

That's when I wake up and look at my sleeping wife. Her blond hair spills across her pillow like water. She's breathing slow and heavy through her thin lips. The moonlight coming through the window shows her turned-up nose in profile. I look at the ceiling fan which whirs with a low-level electronic hum. We had it installed last week along with crown molding and a chair rail in the dining room. We talked about how pleased we were with it all, how our little condo was coming together. I reach down and check my penis. It's of a normal size that, while not exemplary, has served me fine and has been deemed by Melissa to be of adequate proportions.

✳✳✳

That morning, Melissa is in the kitchen, and I'm sitting at the table eating cereal. "Everything okay?" she asks.

"Yeah. Why?" I ask looking down at my bowl.

"You're quiet."

"I'm tired. Didn't sleep so well."

I'm trying to make sense of that horrid dream and figure out what Frida and Diego are doing in my subconscious. The best I can come up with is that while downtown for a conference, I'd gone to a museum on my lunch hour and seen a Kahlo self portrait. Also, I'm a little backed up. Melissa and I aren't fighting, but we're not fucking much either. We're stuck in some sexless coexistence. I'm thinking things are just cooling off the way everyone jokes that they do after a few years of marriage, though I have this nagging fear there's something larger looming in darkened corners. Frida crept into my head at the wrong time. "I'm sorry you're not sleeping, honey," Melissa says. She brings me a cup of coffee and kisses the top of my head in a gentle and caring way that makes me hate myself for dreaming of Frida Kahlo masturbating. I finish my cereal. I go to work. At work, I spend hours reading about Frida Kahlo.

✳✳✳

Melissa isn't home when I return that evening. She texts me a few minutes later: "Grabbing drinks with people from work."

"Have fun. See you soon." I write, but really, I'm wondering who is there because she works at this consulting firm that likes to hire tall, good-looking frat boys with broad chests, fantastic hair, and way too much self-confidence. Also, it's June, a time of year when inappropriately dressed female interns invade D.C. offices causing some of the established professional women to shorten their skirts in a type of sexual arms race. Melissa's hemline hasn't changed. Still, hormones are in overdrive all over the Farragut and Dupont neighborhoods. Downtown turns into an incubator for lust and desire. Meanwhile, I spend my days in a basement cubicle in Wheaton.

Melissa comes home around nine. I kiss her expecting to smell faint remnants of vodka. Instead, I smell red wine, her perfume, and her sweat. She never orders wine at bars, and I wonder if she went to happy hour at all.

"Where did you all go?" I ask.

"Big Hunt," she says. "Half-price burgers."

"And red wine?"

"I'm classy," she says.

***

That evening, Frida puts her hand on the top of my head. "Rodillas," she says, and she pushes me to a kneeling position. She wears a long, black, wool skirt embroidered with flame-red stitching that swirls and moves. She lifts her dress slowly exposing platform red canvas boots with intricate beading in the shape of two roses along the outsides. The boots go all the way up her calf and I trace their contours, one boot in each hand, until I get to the tops and touch her skin just below her knee. She lifts her skirt to her waist and reveals an impressive growth of untamed pubic hair extending down her thighs. The unruly hair reminds me of her defiantly robust eyebrow. I look up at her, and she looks down at me. A sinister smile spreads across her bright red lips. I continue moving my hands up her legs, over her knee and up her thighs. Then, the skin under my left hand, Frida's right leg, shrinks and wilts. It feels dead and wooden. Fissures emerge. I see a small worm crawl out of her timbered skin. I look up into Frida's dark brown eyes. Her smile grows hard. "Polio leg, muchacho. It's nothing," she says, and places her hand on the top of my head stroking my hair with her long, delicate fingers. I'm thinking she's comforting me, that she senses my unease. Maybe she's self-conscious, and she'll guide me through this sexual exploration gently.

Instead, she pulls me forward violently and shoves my face

into her crotch. "Tiempo para comer," she says. She pushes me hard into her pubis. I can't orient myself or open my mouth. She smells earthy and musty. Her pubic hair rubs my cheeks hard like a stiff paint brush. I try to pull away. She laughs, pushes me harder into her crotch, and grasps my head with her thighs. In this struggle, I breath heavy and inhale the full scent of her vagina. The smell is putrid and alluring at the same time, like a naked withered leg underneath a long beautiful skirt. I want to taste it, good or bad, for the experience of knowing that famous vagina completely. This is important. This is living.

I wake up.

***

I watch Melissa dress for work in a black pencil skirt and light-blue blouse. She's looking into the mirror above her dresser and adjusting her bangs. Her blouse tucks neatly into her skirt and she cinches it up with a black, patent leather belt. Her black shoes have just enough heel to be sexy but are low enough to be professional. She catches me looking at her and smiles.

"You should try that hair gel I got you," she says. "I think you'd look handsome."

"I'm afraid I'd look like a politician." The thought of that gel, of the word "handsome" makes me feel like I should put on some Aqua Velva, shave with a straight razor, and use a money clip.

"There are worse things," says Melissa.

"There are, but I don't want to look like those either."

She rolls her eyes and looks back into the mirror.

I'm wearing my weekday uniform of a shirt, tie, and slacks. The colors rotate daily, but it's all the same. I feel like I'm pretending at being an adult.

"I just think, you know . . ." she circles her hand at me and I look down at my Dockers and worn brown shoes, ". . . you could work this better."

It's true. I could. I wonder if the guys at her office wear hair gel. Maybe it's a thing, unlike Dockers. Maybe I should step up my game, be the hottest guy in a basement cubicle in Wheaton.

We walk down East-West Highway toward the Silver Spring metro. A motorcycle whizzes by at an alarming speed, engine thundering, weaving through the heavy traffic. Blond hair whips wildly out the back of the cyclist's helmet. She's wearing a black tank top and has bare, tattooed arms and shoulders. She passes quickly as if she were never there at all, an inked apparition.

"What a fucking psycho," Melissa says.

"Yeah," I say, and I wish I knew who she was and how to find her again. I'm thinking of Melissa's ass in that pencil skirt mixed with the disheveled hair and tattoos of the biker and all of it seems equally attractive and unattainable. I turn and look at Melissa who is looking DC-professional-sexy, and can't figure out why we aren't fucking like crazy. I wonder if it's my fault. I wonder if it's hers. I wonder if it's Frida's. I wonder if hair gel can solve it.

That evening, Melissa's next to me in bed reading some briefing. I lean toward her to kiss her and she tilts her head to offer her cheek. She doesn't take her eyes off her stapled papers. In case I hadn't made my intentions clear, I lean in to kiss her again, this time stroking her hair as I do it, and she says, "I've got to read this tonight, okay?"

"Okay," I say, and lay on my back on my side of the bed staring up at the ceiling with its beautiful crown molding. I know something's wrong, and I know part of what's wrong is that I'm eager to go to sleep and see Frida.

✱✱✱

Soon, I'm in a dark room, and in the distance I see a man in a suit sitting in a chair. I approach, then realize the figure is not a man. It's Frida, her hair cut short, her mustache more prominent than ever. I recognize this Frida from her painting *Frida Chops her Hair* which causes me to look down. Sure enough, I see black hair strewn across the floor. "Hola, muchacho," she says in a deep voice. A glint of light attracts my eye to the silver scissors she's holding in her lap. "Diego left me," she says, "but he is just a boy anyway. Renacuajo." She motions for me to approach with a single commanding finger, and I obey. I stand in front of her, and she looks up at me smiling. Her black mustache accentuates the sharp red of her painted, full lips. She puts her hands on my hips, her right hand still holding the scissors. I hear a quiet hissing sound and look toward the floor. The locks of hair are alive and writhe about like small black snakes. She sees me looking at them, then slaps my ribs. "Don't pay attention to them. They're only symbolic. Original sin and all that." I refocus and lock eyes with her. She leans back and slouches in her chair and with her scissors, she rubs her crotch over the exterior of her suit pants. It's dark, and I can't be certain, but I think she has an erection growing. With her other hand, she reaches into her jacket pocket, pulls out a flask, and takes a big swig.

I hear a muffled whimpering in the dark recesses of the room. I look for its source and see Diego in the shadows crying. His chubby cheeks glisten with tears. He's shirtless and his ample breasts and stomach look soft and supple. His pink areolae are the size of tea saucers and his nipples are dark and prominent.

"Be quiet, Diego!" Frida yells. His whimpers subside for a moment but start up again.

"He is weak sometimes, and he needs me to take charge," Frida tells me.

I can see now, as she says this, that she does have a penis. It's full and erect, its outline showing clearly beneath her slacks.

"Are you scared?" she asks, her eyebrow twisting to convey uncertainty.

"Yes," I say.

"Por que? El pene?" She laughs and hands me her flask. "Big sip," she says. "It is only a pequeña diferencia."

Diego's still whimpering. The hiss of the snakes transforms into a chortle echoing Frida's bemusement. I hand the flask back to Frida. She holds it to her lips for a long time, lifts it high, then drops it to the floor. Snakes scatter. She sits up again and puts her hands on my hips. She unbuckles my belt. The sound of the buckle heightens my anticipation and fear. Then, she turns me around. She pulls my pants down slowly and says, "Today, I am the muchacho, and you are the señorita, eh?" She reaches around me and runs her pointer finger down the length of my penis one time, and I'm erect. My heart beats fast through my whole body, through my cock, which she rubs gently again as she whispers, "There, there, muchacho. Don't worry so much."

She runs a finger down my lower back all the way to my anus. She circles my hole with her finger tip, then shoves her finger into me.

✳✳✳

I wake up with a gasp, and see Melissa sleeping next to me. I look at the new ceiling fan. I look at the floor and see the beige carpet I vacuumed yesterday. I'm oriented and starting to feel better until I realize my boxers are wet. I came while dreaming about a male Frida Kahlo.

Melissa enters the kitchen. I'm drinking coffee at the table.

"You were up early," she says.

"I woke up and couldn't get back to sleep, so I hopped in the shower."

She smiles at me and walks over to the coffee maker. She's wearing short shorts, and as she walks away, I make a point of admiring her ass. I think of all the heterosexual things I've done to it and all I'd like to do to it in the future. I feel my penis growing, a wonderful affirmation of my sexual orientation.

"Melissa," I say, "You're working those shorts."

As soon as it's out, I regret saying it. She doesn't say anything or turn around, but does a little hip shake while reaching for the coffee pot. I laugh, but it dies quickly. We have nothing to say to keep this going.

Melissa sits down across from me with her own cup of coffee. I smile. She looks at me, and says, "What's wrong?"

I exhale. I consider telling her nothing is wrong. I consider making something up, telling her I'm thinking about work, but

I'm pretty sure I've already paused long enough for Melissa to recognize any lie I tell as a lie. I consider telling her I think the guys at her office, particularly Jake, all want to fuck her, that I think maybe one of them actually is fucking her, that I can't talk to her anymore, that we're not having sex, that we're not talking about anything beyond ceiling fans and crown molding, that I don't want to wear hair gel, that our whole marriage has dissolved into polite exchanges and a careful division of household chores. After considering all this, I say, "I've been having a lot of sex dreams lately."

"Oh yeah? Tell me about them," she says, and she strokes my side which is meant to be sensual but instead feels awkward and ill-timed.

"Not like that," I say. "They're not really sexy."

"What do you mean?"

"They're sexual, but uncomfortable. They turn me on, but they're gross."

She puckers her face and leans back. I tell her about the Frida dreams in a general, big picture way. I leave out the homosexual parts.

"That's pretty strange," she says and gives a short, quick exhalation like a forced half giggle.

"I know. And it's turning me on, but at the same time they're weird, horrific, and disgusting."

"Like how?"

I tell her about the polio leg.

"That's pretty sick," she says.

"I know, but I kind of like it." I say this knowing it'll make her uncomfortable.

She shrugs her shoulders, then stands up. "I should get changed," she says. "Time to get going."

We walk to the Silver Spring metro and board red line trains moving in opposite directions.

✱✱✱

The next evening before bed, Melissa tells me to sit on the

bed for a moment. She goes into the bathroom, then emerges wearing a long teal skirt with cream lace trim, a white blouse, gold sash, several large silver rings, and a wooden-bead necklace. A black wig with red ribbons woven into elaborate braids covers her blond hair. Mascara darkens her eyebrows and joins them in the middle.

"Hola, Señor," she says, and walks toward me with a sultry, hippy walk that Frida, with her bad leg, couldn't preform. I smile, almost heartbroken by her effort. At the same time, she is a grotesque, carnival clown imitation of Frida. She's taking a risk, and if this goes wrong it'll crush her. I know I must summon a respectable erection and see this through.

I sit up on the edge of the bed and smile. She walks over to me, and as she does, it's easier to see through her costume. Whisps of blond bangs sneak out from under her wig. I see the mole on her long, thin neck. She pushes me down on my back and straddles me, her hands on my chest. I smell her floral perfume, so different than Frida's musty odor. She tries a seductive smile, but I see doubt in her eyes. I wonder what she envisions as Frida-like undergarments because this has never been revealed to me in my dreams. I remove her blouse and her long skirt as she kisses me hard and deep. Frida Kahlo wears a new, blue lace set from Victoria's Secret. I run my hands over the lace trim on her ass. I look up at her as she straddles me, her perfect, thin, torso, the black wig spilling onto her shoulders. She is not Frida. She is Melissa with a mascara unibrow, and this is simultaneously the saddest and most beautiful thing she's ever done for me. I appreciate how hard she is trying to appeal to my peculiar perversions. Nonetheless, when she reaches behind her and feels my limp penis, there's no explanation or apology I can give that will make it okay.

She rolls off of me and begins to cry. I stroke her hair and say things like "I'm sorry," and "I can't explain it," but I know it's futile and stupid, and I know if Jake were here, he'd happily pound Melissa silly, probably with an enormous frat-boy cock as thick as my forearm. She's broken, curled up in her powder blue lace underwear. She rubs her eyes, and her mascara eyebrow streaks across her face. I roll over and hold her, but she pushes me away. I retreat to my side of the bed. She shakes when she cries, and I can feel the her trembling body reverberate in the mattress as I lay next to her wanting to sleep, to ignore everything and go to Frida.

***

The only light in the room illuminates Frida's large four-post bed. She lays there, her eyes fixed on photographs of Engels, Lenin, Stalin and Mao set up on an easel at the end of the bed. I approach, and when I do, my feet echo on the cement floor. I can't see the walls in the room, only the bed, a wooden chair, the easel, and darkness beyond. The sound of my feet, however, the way it travels, suggests the space is large and cavernous.

I sit in the chair next to the bed and look at Frida. She doesn't move and stares at the photographs. I don't know if she's aware I'm here. She looks older than the other Fridas I've seen. Her once-taut skin sags and gathers under her chin. Her pronounced mustache looks more matronly than masculine. I wait for her to move. Then, I see a bulge riding underneath her blanket at her crotch. I watch it grow fearing my dream Frida will have a penis from now on. Then, the bulge grows to an impossible height, something I find unbelievable even within this dream construct. I look at Frida's face, and the corners of her lips curl in a smile. Her eyes move to catch me, and she bursts out laughing. She pulls a long paintbrush out from under the blanket and waves it at me. "I had you, muchacho. Had you going." She tickles my chin with the end of the brush. "Pene grande!" she says. She drops the paintbrush to the ground. It makes a loud rattle against the floor and the sound echoes for an unnaturally long time.

She puts her hand on my knee, and says, "I am stuck, muchacho." She pulls down her blanket. A plaster cast decorated with oil paints encapsulates her torso. She's painted a hammer and sickle on her chest along with colorful shapes and zig-zagging lines. "I still make it sexy, no?" She runs her hands over the breasts of her plaster cast tracing her curves slowly and carefully. She wears bright red nail polish that matches her lipstick. Her hands move under the blanket to her crotch, and she spreads her legs, the blanket stretches across her raised knees which move back and forth rhythmically.

"Where is Diego?" I ask. Despite everything, my lust for Frida grows and I don't want him to show up.

"To hell with that sapo," she said. "He is out with one of his putas."

She's silent for a minute and closes her eyes, her hands below the blanket, knees moving back and forth. "It's okay though. I have my own putitos, eh?" she laughs, but it turns into a cough and she stops.

"You're sick," I say.

"Cállate! I am already dead. That is not important. You must help me," she says, and she removes one hand and reaches up to the crack between her headboard and her mattress and pulls out a pair of large scissors. She hands them to me.

"Take off my cast," she says. "I would rather die fucking than stay like this."

She closes her eyes again. I sit stunned, wondering where to begin.

"Rapido!" she yells at me, her eyes still closed.

"Okay," I say. I stand up over her and pull the blanket down to her waist, the bottom of the cast. She sucks in her stomach and pulls the cast out from her body with her hands. "Hurry," she says, and I put the scissors into the space she's created, but they don't cut well through the plaster. I start using them like a flat-toothed saw and gnaw at the plaster. The cast begins to flake and chip. I'm making clumsy, slow progress and Frida is ripping at the cast with her bare hands, grunting. I manage to expose her belly button and the sight of her pale, flat stomach motivates me to work with fever, the ultimate goal being full exposure of Frida's nakedness. I nick her skin at her ribs and the cut oozes blood. "I'm sorry, Frida."

"Psht," she said. "Look at me. You think that cut is my pain?" She continues ripping at the plaster with her hands. I work up to her rib cage smearing her blood over her torso as I go. Finally, I get all the way to her neck line and nick her again, but this time, I don't stop. I tear at the cast with my hands too. The cast gives and opens up like twin cellar doors exposing Frida's torso and bare breasts. Smeared blood and plaster make a messy abstract on the canvas of her pale skin. She exhales, and her chest falls. The motion is an expression of liberation and vitality.

I place my hand on her breast and lean down to kiss her proud neck. She tilts her head back to let me, and moans when I do, but after a moment, she pushes my shoulders. "Basta!" she says.

I sit up, and look at her searing eyes under her powerful eyebrow. "Cerdo, you think we went through all that work so that I could lay on my back for you?" She sits up and pushes me off of her so that I'm sitting on the bed. Then, she gets up on her knees and pushes me on my back. She pulls my pants down, then straddles me. "I may be dead, but I still know more about living than you do," she says. She puts me inside of her and rides me hard and angry, the whole time cursing in Spanish and English. The motion becomes violent until it ceases to feel like sex at all and becomes a transcendental experience through which I'm carrying a massive erection and uncontrollable lust.

I wake up in bed next to Melissa frightened, exhausted, exhilarated, wet with semen and sweat, satiated. Then, I remember Melissa trying to fuck me and having it all go horribly wrong. I remember how bad things have gotten between us.

✳✳✳

Melissa hardly speaks to me that morning. After showering and dressing, she goes to work early which saves us from breakfast together and the walk to the metro. Later, in my cubical, I can't concentrate. I search the web to learn more about Frida. I find nude photographs of Frida which of course lead me to more nude photographs of her, then to models dressed as Frida, nude. Apparently, others share my fantasy. But the perfect models in the crisp color photos, though often more beautiful than Frida, don't hold the same appeal as the yellowed black and whites of the real Frida, defiant with her bare breasts, arm pit hair, eyebrow, and unsettling stare. The models are poor imitations, like Melissa in her powder-blue Victoria's Secret underwear. I know it's not fair to hold Melissa, or anyone else, up to a revolutionary feminist icon like Frida, but to some degree I'm ruled by my penis which made its own frank statement the previous evening. I clear my browsing history upon leaving work.

✳✳✳

I'm sitting on the couch watching TV when Melissa comes home around nine. She stands in the doorway wearing tight-fitting slacks and a simple blouse with thin straps that show her slender shoulders and long neck. Her hair is up, but breaks loose from her hairband in places and brushes her cheeks. I've always known she is beautiful, that I am overachieving. This image of her in the doorway is a striking reminder.

She looks at the floor by my feet, and I can tell she feels compelled to tell me something I won't like. I turn off the TV and wait for her to speak. "I went out to dinner with Jake," she says.

"Why?"

"He kissed me."

"He kissed you? What were you doing, fighting him off?" My outrage and surprise are forced. In truth, I expected her to say something far worse once she stopped in the doorway. Also, at least now there is a specific transgression at which I can direct my anger, and it's not nearly as bad as I'd feared. I'm almost thankful.

"I'm sorry," she said. "Everything is messed up right now."

I wanted to point out that while that was true, I wasn't going around kissing other people. Then, I thought of Frida and realized I didn't have a lot of moral high ground to stand on. I think of Jake, his good hair (gel?), his thick wallet, and I imagine him and Melissa at some DC steakhouse I can't afford with K-street lobbyists at the bar, dim lighting, American flag lapel pins everywhere, and an austere, wood-stained decor. This, more than the kiss, is unpalatably pornographic.

She sits in the rickety futon lounge chair that no one ever uses and puts her work bag down between her feet. I turn to look at her.

"What the fuck, Melissa?"

"I was mad at you, and it felt good to be wanted. And after dinner, he hugged me. Then he gave me a peck. Just a peck, then I pulled away."

"Fuck, Melissa. With that asshole?"

"I know. He is an asshole, but he's trying so hard, and part of me likes that, you know?"

I did know. I think of Melissa emerging from the bathroom with a mascara unibrow and long Mexican skirt. I love her as much as ever which is precisely what makes everything so confounding and unbearable. Frida and Jake are preying on our vulnerabilities, one using a hammer and sickle and a mesmerizing eyebrow, the other using boat shoes and a tailored blazer.

"I'm sorry. It was stupid."

"And what's it going to be like at work tomorrow?"

"Awkward and shameful. I was flirty for sure." She twists the strap of her bag. We sit in silence for a while. "I shouldn't have gone to dinner," she says.

"That's true," I say. " And I'm sorry too."

"What are you sorry for?" she says.

I'm not exactly sure, but it has something to do with Frida, the tattooed woman on the motorcycle, and my limp penis the night before. "Things are bad, Melissa. They've been bad and now they're getting worse. I don't know why, but I know you feel shitty too."

"Why do you keep dreaming of Frida?" she asks.

"I don't know. I'm scared of her but she's also sexy."

"Am I those things?"

I'd never considered it before. "Yes," I say, which is true. Her sexuality scares me.

"Frida is dead you know. She's not real."

"I don't know what's happening."

"I don't think you love me anymore. The kind of person you want . . . it's not me."

I don't know what to say, because she might be right. I think about Jake ogling Melissa in her sexy work clothes the next day in the office. The image of the cubicles, the fluorescent overhead lights, pressed shirts and ties, the smell of the copy machines, the sideways glances, all made me want to hurl. I picture Frida's painting of New York City, her capitalist dystopia, and wonder what she would have painted if she'd visited D.C.

Melissa curls up in that chair, her face buried in her knees and her hands over her face. She cries, her body shaking in rhythm with her sobs.

✳✳✳

That night, I sleep on the couch. Once asleep, I slip into Frida's bedroom amidst darkness and a gray fog. Frida sits in a wooden chair, stiff and so straight that I assume she's wearing her back brace. She rests her feet on a stool and a young, beautiful, bare-breasted woman kneels down and rubs Frida's swollen, misshapen feet. As I approach, the young woman looks up at me, her eyes wide, her features soft and pale, and then she quickly looks back down at Frida's feet.

"Hola, muchacho," says Frida. She motions to a stool next to her that I assume had been used by the young woman before she kneeled down to rub Frida's feet. I sit, and I look at the elegant curve of the young woman's back as she works bent over kneading Frida's deformed feet.

"Do you see her beautiful spine? How it bends and curves, how it leads so beautifully to her shoulders and her neck?"

"Yes," I say. "She is beautiful."

"She makes me jealous though. I hate her some," says Frida.

"You are beautiful too," I say.

Frida whips her head towards me and furrows her eyebrow so that I think lasers may fire from her eyes. "I know I'm fucking beautiful, muchacho. But my spine doesn't work. I'm jealous of that." Her scowl melts and she turns her eyes back to the woman working on the floor. She tilts her head to the side, then says without looking at me. "Why are you here?"

"I don't know," I say. "I never know why I come to you. Usually we . . ."

"I do not need you today. I have her," she says and she nods at the girl on the floor who is now massaging Frida's calves.

"What should I do then," I say.

Frida shrugs. I wish I could leave, but the space is black. There is no room to leave, no door. I hear a garbled voice. I can't make out the words, but I know it's Diego.

Frida rolls her head back and yells "Cállate, rana!"

The voice stops.

"How is Diego?" I ask. I know there were two marriages, one divorce, many affairs, and I'm trying to grasp onto some chronology.

"I hate him. He is everything. I will kill him some day maybe, and when I do, it'll be the most heartbreaking loss any woman has ever known."

She's obtuse and I feel useless sitting next to her unneeded. I garner the nerve to say, "What about me?"

She exhales, then says, "You are a nice boy, and you need me."

This hurts, but it's honest. I know I am no Leon Trotsky.

"You are like her," she says, and she lifts her long skirt and throws it over the head of the woman at her feet. "Ir más alto," Frida commands the woman. I see the shape of the woman moving up to Frida's hips under the skirt. Frida tilts her head back and exhales.

"What should I do about Melissa?" I ask.

"Muchacho, I am busy now," she says pointing to the girl under her skirt. "Love her if you want, hate her, or do both."

Frida moans, then reaches out, squeezes my thigh hard, and shifts her hips. The young woman's shoulder moves rhythmically beneath the skirt. Frida giggles, then says, "que bueno, chicita."

"You must come back another time, muchacho. Go to your esposa. Su matrimonio desordenado."

I slide back into the darkness, stool and all, and I watch Frida grow distant until I sit alone. Then, I wake up.

Melissa emerges from the bedroom dressed for work, a long black dress with white polka dots cinched at the waist with a patent leather belt, her work bag over her shoulder, and a duffle bag in her hand.

"I'm going in early," she says.

"You don't have to. We can talk," I say, though I feel relief at the idea of her leaving.

"I'm staying at Christine's tonight, maybe for a couple days."

"Okay," I say.

A tear forms in the corner of her eye. She turns toward the door then stops, looks at me, and says, "Did you dream about Frida last night?"

"Yes," I say.

She sniffs, and I can tell she's about to cry when she turns to leave and closes the door.

✳✳✳

It's her idea to meet several days later on Free Admission Sunday at the National Museum of Women in the Arts. She texted, "Because I won't cry in public," which I know is true. She is tough as nails when she wants to be. This museum has a Kahlo self portrait. It's the place I'd been to weeks earlier, the museum I blame for the whole mess. I assume that Melissa knows this, and so when I go there, I wait for her in front of the Kahlo painting.

I'm looking into Frida's familiar, defiant eyes and get so focused on the image that I don't notice Melissa until she's right next to me. I turn and see her in profile. Her blond hair is pulled back into a ponytail and loose strands escape and fall over her ear creating a curved line down to her long neck. She's wearing a loose-fitting white tank top and navy blue shorts.

"I admit there's something strong about her," Melissa says, her eyes on Frida.

"That's true," I say, "At the same time, she was riddled with self-doubt, anger, and illness. It's all very complex and contradictory."

"Brooding. Sexy," she says. "Maybe that's what you like?"

"Maybe. I don't honestly know."

"I know what you mean," she says.

"The painting is kinda stiff, don't you think? I mean I'm not an expert, but I don't exactly get it," I say.

"Yeah," she says. "If this were at Eastern Market, I'd probably pass by."

"Melissa," I say, "How are we going to get you back home?"

"I'm ashamed and embarrassed, and I don't think you love me anymore," she says.

"Why would you say that?" I ask. Frida's outward stare appears to mock my last statement. I think of all of my dreams, both heterosexual and less than heterosexual. I remember Melissa's mascaraed unibrow. I try again. "I love you, but I don't know. I think there's something else I want too."

"Is that what she is?" Melissa gives a nod toward Frida.

"Maybe. It's hard to make sense of it."

"I think I liked Jake's attention because it was simple. He was simple. He likes steakhouses, cocktails, and work. He wears blue blazers."

"That's not me," I said.

"I don't think it's me either."

"Are you sure?"

"No," she says. "But I want to come back home."

I turn to look at her and see a single tear growing fat under her eye until it spills down her cheek. A breach in the dam. I face her and hug her. She collapses into me and grows heavy, and in her weight, I feel a release of whatever she'd been carrying. I hold her tight and put my face into the crook of her neck. She's hot and musty from the July heat. Visceral, and messy. We disengage, and she straightens up to look at me. She wipes her nose with the back of her hand.

"Jesus. I'm a mess," she says.

I pull a coffee shop napkin from my pocket and hand it to her. She wipes her face, then gives it back, used and wet. She reaches back to fix her ponytail, and I noticed a tuft of hair under her arms. Not much, but enough so that I know it's intentional rather than an oversight. I try to construct a timeline based on how quickly I suspect armpit hair grows and decide she stopped shaving about the time of the failed mascara eyebrow role play sex night.

I take her by the shoulders and look her in the eyes. In that silence, I'm trying to convey that I want to take her home, quit work forever, and have messy, musty, snot-riddled, tear-moistened sex with her. I want to tell her about Frida's penis and the girl on the motorcycle. I want to tell her I know Jake means nothing, that he is symbolic, an archetype for normalcy. I want to be her Diego: a monster sometimes, a frog, an enormous king, a whimpering woman with bare breasts, and there always, emblazoned on her forehead, part of her mind's eye.

"Do you think we'll be okay?" she asks.

"No idea," I say. "Not in any simple way."

"Maybe we can be messy but okay," she says.

"That sounds promising," I say. I look at Frida's portrait and study her proud, upturned chin and erect posture. She holds a note for Leon Trotsky in her hand, but I know Diego is there too, just not depicted. I wonder if Frida is wearing her brace or the plaster cast under her embroidered blouse and elegant shawl. I know her long skirt covers her withered leg and aching feet. In some of her self-portraits, the back brace is prominent or organs spill out of the artist's body. In this painting, in the heart of Washington D.C., Frida is elegant and collected, her organs firmly in place, infirmities hidden. The painting is partly true and easy to look at. I expect a lot of tourists like its simplicity.

But, I know Frida too well. Her stare is unnerving and fills me with a longing I'm not sure I can ever quench. The painting does not allow for any certainty as to what will happen next.

"Come on," I say. "Let's get on the metro."

We sit next to each other in the train, my hand on her thigh, her head on my shoulder. I listen to the rumble of the train on the tracks as we speed along through the tunnels underneath D.C.'s long, beautifully embroidered skirt.

Melvin's heart beat quickly as he stepped out of the center field gate and began the race along the warning track, not because of his running pace, which was fairly relaxed, but because of what he planned to do. He peered out of the eye slits and through the neck of the giant foam head he wore and looked up at the crowd. A surprising number of fans, twenty-five thousand, had come out for the Wednesday day game, the last before the playoffs. They cheered with a fever reflective of the team's unexpected first-place season and chanted the name of the character he portrayed: "TEDDY!" They were brimming over with excitement and poised to see something magical. Melvin would supply it, even if it cost him his job.

Six years of losing. Over 500 carefully scripted defeats. He'd accepted his lot good-naturedly his first year. Even in year two, though slightly dismayed, Melvin understood the role he'd come to play as the loveable loser. But how long did they expect him to sustain the act? The adoration he enjoyed, which the PR folks milked relentlessly, had grown from pity and had built to a crescendo this season with the help of celebrity commentary and witty video vignettes. By now, a fan's exclamation of "Teddy!" sounded to Melvin like a goading taunt, a reminder of his failures both real and scripted, inside the giant foam head and out.

As planned, Jefferson, Lincoln, and Washington got out to an early lead. Melvin watched their giant heads bob with the strong strides of his colleagues, all of whom, despite their comical costumes, possessed athletic physiques and full, interesting lives.

John, the guy who wore Lincoln, looked like he could put on a uniform and stand next to the athletes in the dugout. He once got the phone number of a beautiful fan while still in costume. Jefferson took the job on a lark after selling his software company at the age of 32, because "What else is there to do?" George Washington's cell phone rang every two minutes if he forgot to silence it, and he always had someone to meet up with after the game. Melvin, slightly pudgy, balding at age twenty eight, had taken the gig while between jobs, between his own apartment and his parents' house, between adequacy and total failure. Slowly, he'd come to wonder if these failures weren't in fact the qualifications the front office had sought out for his role.

Along the right field line, a faux Philly Phanatic appeared from the bullpen and collided with Jefferson and Washington, pushing them to the ground. Then, the green villain threw Lincoln into the dirt as well. The three downed presidents lay there splay-legged, their bodies writhing.

This is where Melvin went off script. He was supposed to take a strong lead, to get tauntingly close to the finish line, only to stop and fix his Usain Bolt-style golden shoe, allowing a last minute Abe Lincoln victory. Instead, Melvin pumped his legs hard knowing that if he got to the red tape finish line quickly, no one would have a chance to obstruct his insubordination. It'd be over before they knew it.

The fans screamed, "TEDDY, TEDDY, TEDDY." Because Melvin had planned a new path for himself, the refrain took on a genuine tone in his head. It helped propel him past the designated spot for his shoe tying, past six years of carefully orchestrated failure, and through the finish line to the group of Nats-clad PR folks.

The fans erupted into a frenzy, cheering more loudly than at any point during the preceding innings. Melvin threw his hands into the air soaking in his triumph. He ripped off Teddy's presidential shirt. As far as he could remember, he'd never won anything, not on his own. Today, he'd changed history in the face of the PR department's careful instructions. Twenty-five-thousand fans applauded his efforts as he pounded his artificially inflated foam chest.

Behind him, Reynolds, one of the president's red-clad wranglers said, "Jesus, Melvin. What the hell were you thinking? You know they'll fire you." Melvin didn't respond. Of course, he knew it.

Over the PA system, Clint, the boy-band-looking MC of the ballpark, barked his amazement, but when Melvin looked to where Clint stood by the dugout and meet his eyes, he saw disdain behind his smile. Terrance, the hyper, dread-locked male cheerleader who worked the stands like a derecho, locked his eyes in on Melvin and shook his head slowly. Melvin shifted his attention to the fans who were on their feet now. He spread his arms wide and soaked in their adoration.

Except, when he looked closer, examined them as individuals rather than a cheering mass, he saw the dissenters. One man, an older gentleman with a score book under his arm, scowled. A dad, standing next to his cheering, screaming son, clapped slowly, softly, but his face held the same disdain as Clint's. Someone yelled, "Why'd you gotta jinx the playoffs, you bum!" Baseball fans are a superstitious lot, and Melvin had expected some backlash. Acceptable fallout.

The cheers died down as the Nats took the field for the bottom of the fourth inning. Reynolds led Melvin off the field as a fan yelled, "If we lose, it'll be your fault, Teddy!"

Melvin took it all. The anger, the chiding, the disbelief, the adoration. Teddy, as they knew him, had died. This wasn't about the team or the front office. This was about Melvin. Empowerment through disobedience, deviation from the script, choosing his own destiny. In his new post-Teddy existence, if he met defeat, it'd be because of his own missteps, and not because of a script, faked injuries, mo-ped mishaps, or Mr. Kool Aid.

"Teddy! Why'd you do it, Teddy?" someone yelled as the cheers died down. Even now on the verge of being fired, Melvin didn't speak inside his costume, but he wanted to. He wanted to tell him that Teddy's win, Melvin's win, marked the end. Good or bad. It was time for something else. Holding on too long is never good. Complacency is poison. It'd almost gotten Melvin, slowly dragging him down as he trotted along the warning track through years of scripted losses. Superstition and tradition never hold up against progress. Melvin hoped those upset now would come to realize that Teddy's victory had to happen. Strong, willful individuals can shape the future as effectively as a well-run PR department.

A rhinoceros burst out of the woods, charged onto the Ohio Turnpike, and stopped in front of their Subaru station wagon. Lenore instinctively straightened her legs and pressed her feet into the floorboards on the passenger side at the same moment Nat slammed on the brakes. The car slid across the pavement and screeched like sound effects from an action movie. No time for her life to flash in front of her eyes, instead Lenore thought *Is this the moment I die? Here with Nat as we crash head-on into a rhinoceros?* Nat lost control and the car careened off the road colliding head-on with an ash tree. The hood crumbled like an accordion and made a sound like a falling drum set. Lenore lurched forward, then snapped backward, her head bouncing against the headrest. Nat's luggage tumbled into the backseat from the trunk in a series of thunks.

She checked her limbs and felt her head for blood and found everything intact. She looked at Nat. He stared out the windshield wide-eyed, but unharmed. The rubber of their tires gave off an acrid smell. Smoke rose from the hood of the car. The radio played on, some female folk singer Nat had discovered during his freshman year of college before he'd had to come home.

"You okay, kid?" she asked. She wanted to reach over and touch his cheek but remembered he was grown.

He blinked. "I think so. What was that, Mom?"

She looked around for the rhinoceros, but couldn't see it. The music played slow and sad. She looked through the windshield and began to wonder if the rhinoceros had been real at all. Then, a giraffe loped across the road and galloped through the field on the opposite side of the highway, its head disappearing over the horizon.

"Unbelievable," Nat said.

The tree they'd hit was the first line of a forest of ash trees. Nat peered into the woods. She looked at his hands in his lap.

He rubbed the pads of his pointer fingers with his thumb nails. When he'd been hospitalized, his fingers had become red and blistered in that spot. Since about age twelve, when she wanted to know if Nat was doing okay, she'd look at this spot and gauge the health of his skin there.

"I think we're fine," she said, then realized how little credibility she had. If a rhinoceros and a giraffe could emerge from the forest, why not a dinosaur?

When he'd left for college the previous fall, Lenore had been both relieved and uneasy. She could no longer look at him and know how he was doing. Months later, he'd had to come home early before Christmas. He could barely bring himself to board the plane. She'd felt she should have known, should have done something earlier.

"Let's just go. Get out of here," he said.

"You think the car's okay?"

"Okay enough."

"You okay to drive?"

"Yeah, Mom, I'm fine," he said with bite in his voice.

"I mean something like that, sometimes you need a moment."

He pulled onto the road and pushed the car back to a cruising rate. The engine made a laborious grinding noise, and Lenore imagined its internal organs scrunched together, yet still trying to whir and turn with the depression of the gas petal. Neither of them spoke for a while. Lenore didn't want Nat thinking about the faulty engine, so she turned up the music. The folk singer crooned on about the futility of living. Then, Lenore said, "You think there's a zoo nearby or something? That there was some breakout?"

"I guess it had to be something like that. Maybe a circus passing through?"

Lenore looked out the windshield and studied the expanse in front of them, scanning the field and the roadway for creatures.

Nat started laughing. She looked over at him and could tell it was genuine, and that made her smile too.

"I mean, a fucking rhinoceros! Can you imagine if I'd hit it? If I'd had to call the insurance company? They'd think fraud for sure."

She saw his smile disappear and followed his gaze out the front windshield. On the side of a road, a Bengal tiger stood over a bloody zebra carcass. Smears of red covered the tiger's nose and face. It yanked a hunk of flesh from the felled body as they passed. Around the zebra, entrails lay over the asphalt. Even passing at high speed, she smelled the iron-rich blood. She'd seen this scene on the television before, the tiger over its prey, but it'd always been in some remote African grassland, pixilated, and distant. Now, as she inhaled the scent of it, watched it play out on the side of the freeway, it made her nauseous.

"What's going on, Mom?" he asked.

"Maybe the radio will say," she said. She switched on an A.M. station trading the morose female folk singer for the deep, staccato voice of a male news reporter. According to the news, an exotic animal collector had opened his pens and cages, then shot himself in the head. The police had tracked and killed nearly 30 animals already, but more work was needed. "Residents are advised to stay inside. If you are out on the roads near Garrettsville, do not get out of your vehicle."

"No, shit," said Nat. "I don't want to end up looking like that zebra." He sped up. The groan of the engine grew louder. Nat reached over and turned down the radio's volume. "That doesn't sound good," he said.

"It's probably fine," she said. She didn't want to stop, didn't want to be still when the next beasts emerged.

His right hand rested on his knee and he rubbed his finger with his thumb.

"We'll get it checked out this afternoon when we get to Oberlin," she said, and reached over to turn the radio back up.

"Guy must have been nuts to do that," said Nat.

"You shouldn't say that. You never know what goes on with people," Lenore said.

"Mom, he collected tigers and rhinos and then shot himself in the head. That's some next level crazy. Much worse than me."

She turned away from him and looked out the window toward the forest. She studied the space between the trees looking for the next animal. She pictured a big hippo rooting in the grass, biding its time before crashing through the vegetation to terrorize passing cars.

The rattle in the engine transitioned into a rhythmic thunk and smoke billowed out of the mangled hood. "Jesus," said Nat.

"Just keep going. Until we get to the next town," said Lenore.

"It's getting bad, Mom" he said. He had to yell over the din. The smoke grew darker until it streamed out of the hood and traced the front windshield like a running river. Nat leaned forward to see through it as he drove.

"Just slow down some," she said.

His knuckles grew white as his grip tightened, and he pulled himself forward, his chest inches from the wheel.

"Crap, Mom. What are we going to do?"

She flipped the AM radio on again in hopes of better instructions. Maybe the newsman would tell her the police had shot everything dangerous, and that if you happened to be driving down the highway with a smoking, clattering car, it was safe to get out and call a tow truck. Instead, she heard the same repeated news loop she'd heard before.

"Mom, there are flames now."

She looked and saw a slight flicker of orange coming up between the seams in the wrinkled hood. He slowed the car and took it to the shoulder. She imagined herself opening the hood and letting loose flames like spirits exploding from Pandora's box. She'd smother them with a blanket, putting out the fire with heroic confidence. But where did this blanket come from? And once the fire went out, could they drive the car again? Would it be better to die with Nat in an exploding car or to leave the car and get mauled by a zoo animal?

Nat turned off the engine. Without the speed of the car to sweep the flames away, the fire grew. The smoke smelled like oil and rubber. Lenore imagined a maze of engine belts melting into a pool of molten goo.

"Pop the hood," she said, because she still felt like this was something she should do. Lenore walked around to the front of the car. Nat followed, stood next to her, his fists clenched except for his pointer fingers which he worked against the pads of his thumbs.

"We should get away from the car," said Nat.

"I should check," she said.

"Mom. Seriously. Get away."

She pulled open the hood, and when she did, the exposed flames shot toward her, gulping at the influx of fresh oxygen. She jumped back dropping the hood, and hot air shot into her face. The hood made a thud that reverberated in her ears after it had closed. She felt her face, her hair, to make sure she wasn't on fire.

Nat grabbed her hand. "Let's go," he said and led them into the forest. As they left, the rotten smoke chased them. She imagined them in a movie scene fleeing the burning car. The car's fire would reach the gas tank, and the explosion would knock them off their feet but leave them unharmed as they'd barely made it to safety. Instead, she heard nothing, which made her wonder if they'd traded their spot in a drivable car for a forest infested with carnivorous beasts.

"Nat, the animals. We don't know what's out here."

"Well, we're certain of what's over there," he said motioning with his head to where they'd left the flaming car. She looked at him and saw his strong jaw line, stubble on his chin, and his dad's likeness and assuredness. His frailties, she knew, came from her.

Nat walked over to a downed tree, sat, and exhaled. He rested his hands on his knees.

He shrugged. "You got your phone?"

"No," she said. "It's in the car."

"Me too," he said.

"Should we get them?"

"Probably not. Should get to the road though. Someone will see us there."

"Why'd you take us into the forest?"

"In case the car blew up. The trees would give us cover from the debris."

"You thought of that?"

He shrugged.

She heard a guttural hum and turned to see a bushy-maned lion watching them from behind a tree about sixty feet away. It held its head low. Piercing, yellow eyes locked to hers. Lenore stood up, but Nat grabbed her t-shirt.

"Don't run," he said. "You'll make it chase."

Nat kneeled behind a downed log. She stepped backward over it and joined him there. He put his arm around her shoulders to hold her in place. She peeked over the log and saw the lion pacing back and forth, head hanging low, shoulder blades high as if ready to pounce. If it were to pounce, that'd be it, Lenore knew. There would be no running away, no fighting it off. The police would find their picked-over flesh, torn by feline canines, pools of blood soaking into the forest floor. Messy and visceral. A Stone Age end to a modern existence.

"Nat, I love you honey," she said.

"I know, but Mom . . ."

"I always did my best, Nat."

"I know, Mom."

She looked out over the log again. The lion locked eyes with her. It lowered its head and hummed a slow growl. She buried her face into Nat's chest. She could feel his quick heartbeat. In this position, she would await her fate. Either passed over or mauled to death. The lion would decide.

Nat gave a deep exhale, then pushed her off of him. She looked at him expecting to see the unfolding horror reflected in his face. Instead, he appeared stern and composed as he raised his head up over the log and watched the lion.

"Nat, what are you doing?" she asked.

He didn't reply, then stood abruptly and lifted his hands straight into the air.

"Nat!" she yelled, pulling on his pant leg. "What are you doing?"

"Hey!" he screamed. "Hey, lion. Ahhhhhhhhhh!!!!!!"

He waved his arms. The lion lifted its head and its ears shot up straight. Nat stepped over the log and began running toward it. Lenore's first thought was that he'd lost it, that this was the type of irrational behavior his freshman roommate had reported to the University. "Harmful, self destructive." She'd watch the lion rip her son apart. It'd leap, hit Nat's shoulders with its forepaws, knock him down before swiping through his jugular. Blood everywhere.

The lion lifted its head higher as Nat crashed toward it with flailing arms, his heavy feet tramping over the brush and sticks. The lion let out an open-mouthed roar, but Nat didn't stop. He kept whooping and circling his arms. The lion took a cautious step back. Then, with Nat about twenty feet away, it turned and bounded off, its muscular shoulders pushing it through the forest as if it belonged there. Nat stopped running and bent over with his hands on his knees watching it retreat.

Lenore became conscious of her breathing, slow and easy. "How did you know?" she asked. "How did you know it'd work?"

He shrugged. "Seemed logical," he said, "But I wasn't certain."

To her, this wasn't a lot to go on. She worried his heroism came from disregard for his own life. "Weren't you scared?"

"Of course," he said.

A shotgun blast rang out and echoed through the forest followed by a faint roar. Lenore and Nat stayed quiet waiting to hear something else. They heard footsteps coming toward them. A uniformed officer emerged from between the trees. He waved, and they waved back. He came over, shotgun in his right hand. "You all okay?" he said.

"Yeah. Fine," Nat replied.

He wiped his forehead with the back of his sleeve. "Saw your car by the road. You hear what's happening out here?" said the cop.

"We heard," said Nat.

Already, Lenore wasn't looking forward to recounting what'd happened, how she'd stayed crouched behind the log. She wondered what Nat would take away from this, what he'd think of her, what he'd think of himself.

The policeman continued talking to Nat. The officer offered to escort them to the road with the added protection of his shotgun and to give them a ride into town. Nat thanked him, then turned to Lenore. "Come on, Mom," he said. He smiled at her, and they followed the policeman, shotgun swaying at his side.

At some point, he'd get to school. She wanted him to make it through the whole school year, but that seemed ambitious. Last year, he made it two months before the call from dean's office. Nat wasn't eating. Nat never bought books or attended class. Nat's roommate had requested new housing. Still, there had to have been moments, flashes of success, times when he stood up and charged ahead heroically, if not heedlessly. She'd missed them, probably. The dean had missed them. Maybe Nat had too. She imagined him consoling a dorm mate after the loss of a relative or registering voters outside the student union.

They'd both said this year would be better. He'd gone to therapy, gotten new meds. Still, Lenore wasn't confident. At least Nat now knew how bad things could get.

They rode in the police car down the same highway. About a mile on, they saw the rhinoceros that had first caused them to brake. It stood idle in the field, its head down as it rooted through the grass. This time, it looked about as dangerous as an overgrown cow. Lenore thought that if she were to see rhinos all the time, she probably wouldn't be scared of them anymore. It was their unfamiliarity that was frightening.

The policeman saw the beast too. "Looks like the boys still got some work to do."

"How long do you think it'll take?" Nat asked.

The policeman shrugged. "Can't be sure. Bet they'll be a few we don't account for. Get a call in a couple weeks about some sighting or another, but they'll die out."

"I'm sure you'll get them," Nat said. "Now that everyone knows what's happening."

Lenore watched Nat look out the window and saw his dad's strong profile. She looked down at his hands. The pads of his thumbs were red and worn, but he wasn't rubbing them now. Still, she knew he would soon, that the red skin might never get a chance to fully heal. He'd carry that with him. She told herself she'd pay less attention to it.

R.J. looked at his hands folded in his lap and wished he could vanish, escape the room without having to get up and cross it. He raised his eyes and saw John in profile standing with his head bent down and rubbing his forehead with his thumb and forefinger.

"Thought you was on board. Why didn't you tell me you weren't on board?" John said.

"I'm on board. Just in that picture, I don't see it."

"Shoulda said before, R.J."

The blowup photo sat perched on an easel next to the living room couch, prominently displayed for the TV crew that'd just left. In John's estimation, it showed a bigfoot peeking out of a dense forest. R.J. saw the shape, but when put on the spot, he "couldn't be sure" if it was a bigfoot.

John collapsed onto the worn, floral-print sofa, his head tilted toward the ceiling so R.J. could see the underside of his chin. "Christ, R.J.," he said.

"I'm real sorry, John." R.J. wanted things to be like they were years ago, the two of them loading the pickup with a couple of folding chairs, a cooler of beer, binoculars, and a thirty-five millimeter camera. Out there in the mountains, they'd sit for hours talking and joking, letting the beer take hold.

That changed once John got some photos out on the Internet. People had asked him to meet, to speak, to travel to Tennessee for a convention where he and R.J. had shared a hotel room. John at the vanity mirror each night meticulously taking off his watch, stacking his change, taking off his wedding ring, unaware of R.J. watching him, studying the sway of his broad shoulders, the way his hair lay over the tops of his ears.

Then the TV crew. Finally, this.

"It's gonna get out," John said. "It'll get out and people gonna start askin' 'bout you, whether you for real, and 'mma have to answer."

"Say whatcha need to, John. Don't matter to me none."

John exhaled and held his arms wide, palms toward the ceiling. "Thing I wanna know is . . ." He sat up and looked R.J. in the eye. John's eyes looked soft, pleading. "Do you even believe in bigfoot?"

"Think what you did, how you got that website up, talked at that convention and everything, it's remarkable is what it is. I'd follow you to the enda the earth, tell you the truth 'bout it."

"So?"

"Not for me to pass judgement on. Just go along wit you, how I think 'bout it." Fishing, hunting, watching football, anything would have done. John liked hunting bigfoot.

"Hell, R.J. What the hell you been doin' all these years then?"

His eyes bulged and he waited for a response. R.J. couldn't answer, but thought at some point, John would figure it out. He waited for it now, waited to see his eyes soften in realization as he answered his own question. The thought of it frightened and thrilled R.J. But, as much as he liked to imagine John's sudden understanding, he couldn't picture it. It wouldn't come into focus and lurked in the background defying clear identification. He could say he saw it, lay out an idealized version of what would happen next, but he'd be lying. What he saw more clearly was the reality, the here and now, he and John stuck in the living room and him unable to vanish.

The Dragon King's tide jewels gave Princess Tamatori power over the ebb and flow of the sea, but did not cure her loneliness after the death of her husband. Each morning at sunrise, with the tide low, she walked on the beach in hopes of seeing the sea god Isora or the Dragon King himself. Both had access to the underworld where her husband dwelled, and she hoped to barter for his life with the tide jewels.

The morning ritual gave her hope and solace at first, but as time passed, the walk became a source of frustration.

"Isora! Dragon King!" The Princess yelled to the waves one morning, "I am here! I have the tide jewels to return to you." Only the caw of birds and the rumbling of the waves returned her calls.

The next day, she waded into the water up to her ankles. She tried again. "Isora! Dragon King! I have the tide jewels to return to you." Again, nothing.

The next day, she waded in further, hiking up her kimono and wading in so that the water lapped against her bare thighs. The cold water gave her goose bumps and hardened her nipples. She yelled, "Isora! Dragon King! I have the tide jewels to return to you." This time, she felt something swim by and brush the inside of her thigh. She reached down to grasp it, but it slithered away.

The next day, she removed her kimono and waded into the water even further. The water felt cold on her naked breasts and made her nipples hard and red. She yelled for the two gods and felt something slimy pass by and brush against her thighs and return again, over and over, always escaping her grasp. The same thing brushed the length of her back. She saw tentacles floating close to the surface. An octopus. She tried to grab it, but could not catch hold. She yelled out, "Isora, please, let my husband return to me." The octopi swam away, and while part of her felt relief, part of her missed their caresses and Isora's attention.

The following day, Princess Tamatori again shed her kimono and waded into the water carrying the dragon's tide jewels. When the octopus came swimming by, its tentacles teasing her naked body, slipping between her thighs and caressing her nipples, she threw one tide jewel into the water. It floated slowly down. Then, the earth shook. A bang exploded through the air like a hundred claps of thunder. The waters receded and Princess Tamatori fell backward onto the seabed.

She lay naked on the wet, seaweed- and shell-laden sand which had been covered by the ocean moments ago. Dozens of octopi sat nearby. One of them with bright purple spots said to her, "You have uncovered us and we can no longer hide in the water."

"Yes, and I think you've been sent by Isora. I want my husband back."

"Isora will not release your husband from the underworld," said the octopus, "but he will allow us to cure your loneliness." With an arm, he motioned to the octopi around him.

"How can you cure my loneliness, octopus?"

The purple-spotted octopus crawled toward her. Its tentacles tickled her bare toes. "I have skills bestowed upon me by the sea god Isora, and I can make you forget for a moment." He moved a tentacle up the inside of her thigh.

"What are you doing, octopus?" she asked

"Curing your loneliness with all of the cunning tricks afforded me by the sea god Isora," it said, and it slid a tentacle further up her thigh and inside her secret cave. Her body stiffened and she tilted her head back in ecstasy.

"You see?" said the octopus. He continued to probe her and pleasure her. Then, he said, "friends, assist me." Several other octopi crawled toward her. One parted Princess Tamatori's lips and teased her tongue with a delicate tentacle. Another grabbed her nipple with the suction cup on the underside of its limb. A third octopus looped an arm around her neck and pushed gently so that she gasped for breath. All the while, the purple-spotted octopus moved up and put his mouth over her ripe fruit. It sucked vigorously with its slimy mouthpart. The octopi worked together to bring the princess pleasure over and over until she finally yelled, "enough! I am tired and defeated. You have ravaged me and I am satiated." She lay panting, naked, and unmoving on the dry ocean floor.

The purple-spotted octopus said, "That is Isora's gift to you, but it is only for you."

"Please thank Isora. You and your friends made me forget my husband for a while, and I am grateful."

When she regained her faculties, Princess Tamatori stood up, recovered the tide jewel, and returned home.

From then on, Princess Tamatori's morning ritual changed. She no longer called for Isora to bring her husband back from the underworld. Instead, she'd disrobe, wade into the ocean, throw in her tide jewel, and succumb to the pleasures bestowed upon her by the octopi. Each time afterwards, the same octopus would remind her, "This gift is for you, but it is only for you."

This went on for several weeks and Princess Tamatori's happiness increased. She no longer pined for her dead husband. The sexual pleasures overshadowed her grief.

A short time later, her dead husband's brother became ill. Everyone came to his bedside to pay respects. When he died, Princess Tamatori invited his widow, Taira, to live with her by the seaside. Tamatori wanted to help Taira in her grief and hoped the two of them could grow old together, a friendship to cure loneliness.

However, grief-stricken, Taira would not get out of bed. Tamatori expected as much at first. She made Tiarra soup, she read to her, she played the koto for her, and still, after several months, she could not cure Taira of her deep sadness.

Princess Tamatori knew the promise she had made to Isora, but she also remembered what it had been like to be lonely the way Taira was now.

One morning, Princess Tamatori said to Taira, "Come with me, and I will cure your sadness. I will take you to Isora, the sea god. He cured my heartache and he can cure yours as well."

Tamatori took Taira to the beach. "Come, Taira. Let us walk along the beach," said Tamatori. They walked together. "Come, Taira. Let us dip our toes in the cool saltwater," said Tamatori. And they did. "Come, Taira. Let us shed our kimonos and wade into the water. It is the best way to give ourselves to the healing power of Isora."

"I am skeptical," said Taira. "Who will see us?"

"No one is here," said Tamatori. "The closest village is a distance away. You must trust me. I was once sad like you, but now I am not. Do as I say and swim naked in the waves."

Taira entered the water slowly. "It is so cold," she said.

"Come out further so Isora can see you," said Tamatori.

Taira did as she was told. Tamatori threw the tide jewel into the water. The earth shook, and the ocean receded leaving the two naked women on the sandy ocean bottom among the octopi. Then, the octopi pleasured them. Taira's moans and gasps echoed across the sea floor and against the cliff sides. Afterward, she said to Tamatori, "I am satiated. And in that moment, I felt no sadness, no heartache."

"I am glad," said Tamatori.

Then, the purple-spotted octopus who had just crawled off Tamatori's pubis said, "Tamatori, I told you this gift was for you only."

"Forgive her!" pleaded Taira. "She was trying to cure me. It is my fault."

"Isora will not like this," said the octopus, and then it buried itself in the sand.

Taira said, "Tamatori, I hope you are not in trouble. It was a kind thing you did to share with me."

"Don't fret," said Tamatori. "It is only an octopus. I have met Isora himself years ago. He will tell me himself if he is angry." Tamatori wasn't sure if this was true, but it made her feel better. She gathered the tide jewel and the two returned home.

The next day, Taira begged Tamatori to take her to the sea again. Tamatori was glad to see her friend wanting to leave the house, so she took her. Again, Tamatori threw the tide jewel, again they received pleasure, and again the octopus warned them they had upset the sea god.

As they walked home, Taira said, "That octopus doesn't know what it's saying. You know the sea god. He is not angry with you. That octopus is not as powerful as you. You hold the tide jewels!"

"Be wary, Taira," said Tamatori. "We don't know how the gods think."

"But you are Princess Tamatori. You stole the tide jewels and you receive pleasure from the sea god each morning. You are like a goddess yourself!"

"I am not so sure," said Tamatori.

The next day, Taira and Tamatori went to the sea again. When they arrived, two other women stood on the beach.

"Who are you?" asked Tamatori.

A young woman with ink-black hair said, "We are from the fishing village. We heard your moans yesterday while gathering reeds for our baskets. We came to the beach and saw you receiving pleasure. Now, we want to receive pleasure too."

"The sea god told me not to tell others," said Tamatori.

"If you do not include us, we will have no reason to keep your secret." said the woman with ink-black hair.

"Just for today," said Tamatori.

The four women shed their clothing and entered the water. Tamatori threw the tide jewel and the four women received pleasure from the octopi. The four of them moaned and gasped in pleasure. For the first time, Tamatori was unable to give up her mind fully to her pleasure because while the octopus probed and sucked her, she worried her screams of delight coupled with those of the other women, might attract the attention of more villagers. Before receding into the sand, the purple-spotted octopus said to Tamatori, "I've warned you over and over, yet you do not not heed my warning. There are more women to pleasure each day. I'm growing weary."

"I'm sorry, octopus. Your powers are great and you've done so much to heal me and Taira. Word of your great work has traveled, and I'm worried I have lost control of your secret."

"I have done what Isora has asked. I have also done a little more, and you have taken advantage."

"I'm sorry, octopus."

The octopus crawled away and buried itself in the sand.

Tamatori gathered Taira and the two other women. They stood before her naked and unashamed, heads high, backs straight, smiling, cheeks flushed, hair mussed, and skin glowing.

"I am glad you enjoyed the pleasures of the octopi," said Tamatori, "But you mustn't come again, and you mustn't tell anyone else. The sea god Isora will become angry."

"Posh! Who are you to hoard this pleasure?" said the woman with ink-black hair. She was young and her small nipples were still red and hard from the suction of the octopus.

"I am Princess Tamatori! I have commanded an army, tricked the Dragon King, stolen the tide jewels, and cavorted with the sea god."

"And now you command us?" asked the woman. "You look old and tired. And now you are begging."

"I ask of you."

"You are not so great," said the woman. "Besides, I am certain the octopi liked me best. I have the sweetest secrets to unveil, fresh and new secrets, while your cave is old and used up. You are jealous of me."

"I ask you please," said Tamatori, but the two women only walked away. Taira and Tamatori left as well.

The next morning, Taira woke Tamatori. "Sister, wake up! Let us go to the seaside again."

"Let us stay home this morning, and for a few days until others grow tired of waiting and cease to come out to the beach."

"Nonsense!" said, Taira. "I am lonely and aching. I must see the octopi today, or I may swell with loneliness."

"Can you not quell this swelling on your own, in some other way?" asked Tamatori.

"There is no comparison to the pleasure sea god Isora offers."

Tamatori knew this to be true, and while she thought it best to stay away from the beach, she herself felt lonely and wanting. She'd grown too accustomed to visiting the octopi each morning.

When they arrived at the beach, the two women from the day before stood among the reeds where the vegetation met the sand. One of them spotted Tamatori and pointed at her. The two walked toward Tamatori and Taira, and then four other women emerged from behind the ridge and followed.

Tamatori said to the woman with ink-black hair, "I told you not to come and not to tell others. Now there are four of you."

The women took off their kimonos and stood before her naked, their breasts pert and youthful. "Shut up, old woman," said the woman with long ink-black hair. "Throw the tide jewel into the ocean and make us scream and moan."

"You will anger the sea god. You will ruin everything."

"Can you see I am naked and ready?" said the ink-black haired woman.

Taira tugged on Tamatori's arm. "Tomorrow we will stay at home, but we are here now. These women are disrespectful, but we should not let it ruin our fun."

Tamatori looked around at the women before her. The woman with ink-black hair scowled, her eyes burning, and she held her hands on her hips. Tamatori turned and threw the jewel in the sea. The tide receded.

Dozens of octopi emerged. They crawled over Tamatori and the other women like an invading army. The octopi knocked them on their backs, spread their legs, and conquered their hidden spaces with exacting skill. Tentacles slid up necks, around waists, into wanting mouths, around thighs, and in and out so that the women howled and panted. To Tamatori, the pleasure felt greater than on any previous day. Several times she thought it too much, almost wished it to stop, but with each pinnacle of pleasure, she felt release, then new desire. She let the octopi bring her to climax over and over again. Several times Tamatori lost her awareness of her surroundings as the octopi brought her to a place of pure sensation. However, she came back to earth after each pinnacle, and when she did, she could look around the beach and see the other naked women writhing in pleasure, howling and moaning like music unheard of before on earth, a cacophony which traveled the length of the seaside.

After what seemed like hours, the octopi crawled off of Tamatori leaving her exhausted on the beach. The moans and screams of pleasure from the other women stopped as well, and in their silence, Tamatori could hear the calls of the gulls and rumble of the waves.

The purple-spotted octopus said to her, "Now, word has spread of our abilities to bring pleasure. Soon there will be innumerable women here begging me to please them. Something must be done and this is it." The octopus lifted a tentacle and pointed it toward one of the younger women lying naked on the beach, an octopus still on top of her. The octopus curled an arm around the girl's neck. She gasped, not a gasp of pleasure, but a gasp for breath. Her gasps became frequent and hurried.

"Please," said Tamatori. "That octopus is strangling her."

"Yes, and her friends will hear about it," said the purple-spotted octopus. "Word will spread."

Tamatori got up and took a step to run toward the young woman, but the talking octopus grabbed her ankle. "You can't rescue her. There are too many of us and we have the powers of Isora."

Tamatori knew this to be true, and all she could do was watch as the octopus strangled the last breaths out of the young woman. When it was done, the octopus crawled off of the young woman and retreated to the sand.

The purple-spotted octopus said to Tamatori, "Do you remember why you started coming here?"

Tamatori only looked at him wide-eyed. The other women, frightened by the murder of the young woman, gathered around and listened.

"To cure my loneliness," said Tamatori.

"Not exactly. You wanted your husband returned from the underworld," said the purple-spotted octopus.

All the octopi scurried off. Then, on the horizon beyond the waves, Tamatori saw a figure emerge. It walked toward her, and she recognize his gait as that of her husband.

"Look! It is Prince Fuhito!" Taira yelled. All of the women, even those who'd never met Prince Fuhito, felt relief in the sudden rebirth after the young woman's death. They ran toward Fuhito. When they reached him, the woman, still naked, all hugged him, tears in their eyes. Tamatori hugged him and kissed him as well and said, "My love, you have returned to me." He smiled back at her in a vacant way, a distant look she now remembered he often gave shortly before he died. She noticed the wrinkles at the corners of his eyes. The husband she'd been remembering had been younger, strong and virile. This Prince Fuhito was old and weary.

Nonetheless, he was back, and she loved him. The other women continued to shower him with kisses and pressed their naked bodies against him. He smiled and after a while, the women disengaged and let him walk on, which, Tamatori noticed, he had no problem doing. Despite their attentions, there was no bulge at the crotch of his pants.

The next day, Princess Tamatori made tea for her husband. They discussed the fine morning and marveled at the garden. Taira joined them and said, "Prince Fuhito, it is so nice to have you back. Your wife suffered in your absence and had grown quite lonely."

He gave a kind smile of the type elders give, and he placed his hand on top of Tamatori's. She did her best to be content with her husband's sweet companionship: their evening strolls, their reminiscing, their time together in the garden, and her playing the koto for him.

Still, in the mornings when she woke up next to him, she thought of the octopi. Often, she pulled the blanket off of her husband in hopes that in his sleep, his staff had awoken. Most often, his robes lay flat. However, one morning, his robe billowed out and Princess Tamatori, in a fit of excitement, straddled him and put him inside her. Her husband's eyes opened wide, and he said to her, "What are you doing?" Then, his staff shrank and withered. She looked at his shocked, wrinkled face, felt impossibly old, and began to cry. "But I love you Fuhito."

He stroked her hair, but that was all he could manage.

The next day, Tamatori went to the beach. She threw the tide jewel into the water, and the water receded. The octopus came and said, "What do you want now?"

"I have missed you."

"You have missed the pleasures I brought."

"That is true."

"I gave you what you wanted."

"Yet you knew it was cruel, didn't you?"

"I had an idea," he said.

"And yet you did it anyway?"

"What should I have done? I tried to distract you, but you only created more work for me. I relented and granted your wish."

"That is true," she said. "And yet you've created an ache that can not be healed."

"That ache was of your creation, Princess."

"I suppose you're right," she said. "And you have given me my dear husband, whom I love. How do I reconcile this with my remaining desire? What can I do?"

"Well," said the octopus, "It's clear to me."

"What's the answer?"

"When I wanted to give you utmost pleasure, I brought in many octopi to help me. You, princess, will never be satisfied by your once-dead husband, and I will no longer help you. You will need another man, one who is talented and sturdy."

"Am I not too old for that? I am aging too. I am not like these young women."

"You are wise and full of guile. That is more beautiful than youth."

Princess Tamatori threw the second tide jewel into the ocean. The water returned high on the beach, and she began to walk home. She passed a young fisherman patching nets on a nearby rock. Naked from the waist up, the sun had browned his lean arms and shoulders. She stopped in front of him. He looked up, clearly unnerved to see a princess before him in such a fine kimono.

"Do not be alarmed," she said. "I want to help you."

"You do?" he said.

She looked toward his lap and noticed the outline of a proud staff with a thickness of an octopus arm underneath his pants. "I can help you catch many octopi," she said. "You won't need to patch that net."

"I won't?"

"No. Grab your biggest basket, and I will make sure you can fill it."

"I will be rich! How can I thank you?"

She opened her kimono and walked toward him. "You will pleasure me so skillfully the sea god himself will be jealous of your handiwork."

Lyndon dropped ice cubes into his tumbler, and Heather snapped her head toward him at the sound. He poured the Jack Daniels anyway, took his drink to the dining room table, and laid out his new shotgun, gun oil, and cleaning brushes. He removed the barrel of the gun just as the man at the gun shop had shown him. It didn't need cleaning, but if he didn't go through the procedure today, he'd forget it. He felt Heather's eyes on him from her spot on the couch.

"I still don't see why you need that," she said pushing her bangs off her forehead. She'd let her blond highlights grow out since the move.

"We live in Montana now. We need it for safety. Especially in the winter."

Lyndon wasn't sure what this meant, but several locals had told him as much. He envisioned a scenario where he'd wake up one snowy morning to find a grizzly pawing at the sliding glass door. In another fantasy, snow covered the roads and he took down a moose for sustenance. Afterward, Heather would gaze into Lyndon's eyes and notice for the first time the kind of man he'd become here.

Heather picked up the Larry Watson book in her lap. He'd asked her to come along to the gun shop, but she'd declined like she had when he'd asked her to come look at canoes the week before and fishing reels before that. She extended her legs and pulled a blanket over her bare feet. For her, assimilation meant reading western novels.

They'd moved to Flathead Lake just as the snow began melting into thin streaks alongside the highway. Lyndon had sold his company shortly after his fiftieth birthday. They'd bought a grand house on an underdeveloped inlet, a long-deserved rest after two decades building a company. Lyndon's doctor had said the change would help his hypertension. Heather also wanted something new. So far, Lyndon drove into town to buy things and drank too much. Heather slept late and read on the couch.

He finished cleaning the gun, reassembled it, and looked through its scope. He walked out the sliding glass door to the back deck, drink in one hand, gun in the other. He stood against the rail overlooking the downslope of the hill which met the lake a hundred yards away. Lyndon set his tumbler on the rail and took in "the beautiful view." That was what they called it. They talked about it with pious reverence, and when they did, it helped validate their decision to come to Montana. It was the one thing they agreed was pure and good. When they'd first looked at the house, Lyndon had imagined Heather happy and smiling as she stood on the back deck and gazed out over the lake under the setting sun.

Lyndon lined up the crosshairs with several rocks and leaves. The man at the store had warned him about the gun's "kick." He imagined what that would feel like and pretended to fire at an imaginary bear in the distance.

Heather slid the door open. Lyndon turned toward her. "I'm going to bed," she said.

"Goodnight," he said.

She didn't move. "Lyndon, do you think we could invite friends to visit?"

"Sure."

"Maybe Pete and Lisa? It's not too far for them."

He shrugged. "Ask them."

"Are you coming to bed soon?" she asked.

"In a bit," he said. She turned and left.

He looked through the glass door into living room, then lifted the gun and peered through its scope. He lined up the crosshairs with objects in the house: the vase on the table, the top of the barstool, the framed wedding picture on the side table, then the spot where Heather had sat moments before. He pulled against the trigger, just enough so he could feel the pressure of it. He imagined the loud blast, debris scattered about the house. The fantasy shook him, and he put the gun down and slugged the remaining whiskey. Tomorrow, he'd put the gun deep in a closet.

The next morning, Lyndon stood on the back deck again taking in "the view," this time with a cup of coffee. The rising sun felt warm, a sign summer would arrive soon. Vacationers would flood the town, he'd been told, and renters would fill up vacant houses. Motor boats and jet skis would churn up the silent, flat water. For the first time since buying the house, Lyndon imagined himself actually in the lake, swimming through "the view." Something so pure would doubtlessly have a cleansing effect.

He went inside. Heather sat at the kitchen counter, and he called from behind her. "Heather, I've decided I'm going to swim the inlet each afternoon. And less drinking."

She brushed her brown curls away from her face, turned toward him, and smiled. Lyndon noticed she'd stopped wearing earrings. "Sounds good," she said.

He recognized her effort, and with her smile, his statement became a crucial pledge. He walked over, put his hands on her cheeks, and kissed her forehead. She wrapped her arms around his hips, pressed her head into his chest, and held on like she wanted something.

"Why don't you do it with me?" he asked.

"I'm a horrible swimmer."

"Just to do something together."

"Lyndon, I don't want to," she said and let go of his waist.

That afternoon, he jumped into the lake. His muscles tightened in the cold water. He wanted to scamper back onto the dock, but saw Heather watching from the deck. He treaded water until he warmed up, then set off for the other end. He tired quickly but floated on his back some to rest. Eventually, he made it to the dock where Heather stood holding his towel.

"You did it," she said. He toweled off. She hugged his still-damp body and held on a beat longer than he'd expected.

He looked down at her, but she wouldn't meet his eyes. "Is everything okay?" he asked.

"Yes," she said. A tear formed in the corner of her eye.

He kept the routine going, but Heather stopped coming down to the dock. By June, Lyndon became stronger and added a second loop to the swim, then a third just to show himself he could. Heather plowed through Lonesome Dove in a week and began a Cormac McCarthy book.

"The county fair starts Saturday. It's got a rodeo," he said.

She didn't say anything, only shook her head, her eyes on her book. A doctor in Whitefish had prescribed medication, but Lyndon didn't think she was taking it.

"Did you get hold of Pete and Lisa?" he asked.

"They can't come. They said maybe next summer."

"Well, that's okay," he said. Heather didn't reply.

Lyndon began his evening swim mid-afternoon now, and it lasted for hours. He stopped counting laps by July and ended his swims when his body gave out. One evening, after drying off, he sat on the couch examining the wrinkles on his fingertips. Heather asked him, "Is everything okay?"

"Yeah. Fine. Why?" he said.

She smiled back at him. "It's just a lot."

"I don't drink anymore."

"That's true, but I don't think things have changed much. Do you?"

"No," he admitted. "Is your medication working you think?"

"Hard to tell," she said. "I don't know what it's supposed to do."

"Are you happy?" he asked.

"No," she said.

"Do you think you should see the doctor again?" he asked.

"Jesus, Lyndon. You might want to take a look at yourself. I'm starting to think drinking might have been a healthier pastime."

"You're not making sense," said Lyndon.

"That's an easy explanation," she said.

He got up and went to go get changed. In his closet, he saw

the shotgun. He called back to the living room, "You could swim with me. Remember how you swam everyday in Jamaica?"

"You think that's what I want?"

He walked back to the living room. "I don't know what you want. Tell me."

"I'm tired, Lyndon. I'm lonely."

"We agreed to move."

"I'm stuck with you and all this money." She gestured to the expanse of the house. "I'm a coward."

"Maybe you should see that doctor again, Heather. Maybe the medication isn't right."

"Fuck the medication, Lyndon. Go swim," she said.

Until then, he hadn't noticed swimming had replaced work as his way to leave her each day. She saw through all his dishonesties, even the ones he couldn't see himself, even the ones born out of kindness.

The next morning in the kitchen, Heather said, "I'm driving into Kalispell. I think we need new curtains."

"Great," said, Lyndon.

"Do you want to come?"

"Yes," he said.

"It could be a waste of time. I just want to look."

"It'll be nice to do something together," he said.

It took an hour to get there. In the car, they talked about the color schemes Heather wanted, the house, the changing weather. They went into the store and looked over the displays of curtain rods, pleats, and patterns.

"What do you think of this one?" Heather asked him.

"It's nice. I like it," he said.

She studied his face but didn't change her own expression. She walked toward a salesman. Lyndon pretended to peruse curtain patterns. Heather picked a dark red pattern. Someone would call her soon to set up installation. They drove back toward Rollins, Lyndon at the wheel. They passed a pasture full of buffalo. "Look at that," he said, and she leaned toward the window. "Pretty cool, right?"

"Yeah," she said. "Reminds me of Yellowstone."

They talked about that for a while. They talked about watching flocks of sheep move across open fields during a trip to Scotland and about the pub that had served them a different meal each time even though they'd always ordered the same thing. By the time they reached their mile marker on the highway, Heather was smiling.

Once they pulled off the highway and slipped under the shade of the trees, Heather leaned away from him and into the car door. He switched off the ignition, and they stayed quiet until Heather said, "Let's have a look at that beautiful view," and got out. Lyndon sat there trying to discern whether she'd said it sarcastically.

Two days later, Lyndon put on his swimsuit, went down to the dock, stood in the midst of the mist and listened to the birds. Then, he took off his suit, jumped in, and glided through the water. When he climbed back onto the dock hours later, the mist had burned off. Standing naked, he shook his head and limbs. He dried his feet and noticed the skin between his toes spread out in a thin layer like duck feet. He attributed the change to the prolonged submersion, akin to pruney fingers in the bathtub.

He wrapped up in a towel, walked toward the house, and ascended the stairs to the back deck. Through the sliding glass door, he saw Heather facing a rugged-looking young man in jeans and a flannel shirt holding a curtain rod. Heather laughed. Lyndon slid the door open and when he did, Heather turned to look at him. Her smile faded, and she took a step back from the man.

"Oh, hello," said the man in an unsteady voice.

Heather said, "Lyndon, this is Andy. He's going to install the curtains."

"Great," said Lyndon, and he walked by them into the bedroom. From the bedroom, he heard Heather giggling again.

He always woke up before Heather. He'd read the paper and do some work around the house or yard, but check his watch often to see if he could defensibly go down for his afternoon swim. By noon, he'd feel short of breath and become light-headed, symptoms that vanished when he got into the water.

The doctor checked him out and said there wasn't a thing wrong with him, that he'd developed the heart rate of a pro athlete, though the doctor did recommend lotion for his scaly skin. "There are worse habits," the doctor said. So, Lyndon swam more. Several hours in the morning, then several hours in the afternoon.

Heather put in her diamond stud earrings and drove to a salon in Lakeside to get highlights put in. She wanted to repaint, wallpaper, and renovate the living room with Andy's help.

On the tail end of a hot August day, Heather sat on a barstool facing the kitchen counter as Lyndon fixed himself a sandwich. "What are you going to do once the weather turns?" she asked. He shrugged, trying to hide his panic. "At some point you're going to have to stop, and I'll still be here," she said.

He never tired when swimming. He wished he could extract oxygen from the water like a fish and swim forever. Sometimes, toward the end of a long swim, he found himself wanting to try it, wanting to breathe in the water. A ridiculous, reoccurring daydream.

Lyndon looked past Heather at three paint splotches of different shades of green on the living room wall. "Are you ever going to finish the renovation or should Andy move in?"

"Once I'm done, what will I do then?"

He wanted to say, "Maybe read a western novel," but that would have been petty. Instead he asked, "Are you flirting with him?"

"A little," she said, "but he's fifteen years younger than me."

"Harmless then?" he asked.

"I'm not going to sleep with him, but I wouldn't say it's harmless. It's a desperate grab for attention."

"That sounds dramatic, don't you think?"

"It's sad and desperate," she said.

"Do you think you should see the doctor again?"

"Fuck off, Lyndon," she said.

The leaves changed. Bursts of reds, oranges, and yellows punctuated the landscape. Heather looked out the window and said, "Well, that is a new view, isn't it?"

Lyndon preferred the muted grays, blues, and greens he saw underwater. His skin had changed. Tough scales grew in patches on his body, particularly on his lower back. He hadn't been applying the cortisone lotion as often as prescribed. Spreading out his fingers and toes, he studied the thin webbing growing between each digit.

"I don't see how you can be still be doing that in the cold," Heather said as Lyndon passed through the living room in early November on his way out to the dock. "And for so long."

He stopped and faced her. "I have to. I'm afraid of what'll happen if I don't."

"So am I, I guess. But the lake is starting to freeze. I can see chunks of ice in places." She walked over to the window and looked down at the water. "I mean, you shouldn't be able to."

Lyndon kissed her on the cheek. She looked up at him, her eyes wet, and she put her hand on his chest. "Andy's coming by later to talk about backsplash tiling."

A week later, Heather went to town to look at cabinet hardware, and Lyndon decided to prepare dinner. He found a recipe for stuffed peppers, something he'd made for Heather years ago, and he went to the store for ingredients. The arduous process of chopping and reading and rereading the recipe made Lyndon feel noble.

Heather walked in the front door to a table set with the good dishes, wine glasses, and lit candles.

"What's all this?" she asked him.

"Remember when I made those stuffed peppers when I had that apartment in Redwood City?"

She smiled, walked over, and put her arms around his neck. He took a deep breath and inhaled the smell of her shampoo, the cold air, and fall leaves that she'd brought into the house with her.

"This is nice, Lyndon," she said.

But, he'd undercooked the rice and it crunched as he ate it. Burned black edges marred the peppers.

"It's fine," she said. "It still tastes good."

"Thanks," he said, "but I wanted it to be better."

She told him about the tile she'd picked out, though halfway through her story, he'd stopped paying attention. He listened to the wind and worried about the approaching winter. Soon, they sat in silence, Heather twirling one of her curls around her finger.

By late November, large swaths of ice blocked his path and he swam underwater emerging in unfrozen pockets, darting from spot to spot with ease, twisting his body playfully like a seal. The cold didn't bother him, and he never felt out of breath or worried about coming up for air. Sometimes, he'd see how far he could go without a breath.

His skin dried out more, and the scaly patches expanded. The webbing between his fingers and toes grew more pronounced. His eyes, which worked well under water, took awhile to adjust to sunlight once he emerged, and he saw everything on land through a milky film.

One evening, he and Heather sat in the kitchen: Lyndon at the counter, Heather seated at the table. Heather said, "Something's wrong with you."

Lyndon shrugged.

"You shouldn't be able swim in that cold water. Your hands look odd, and your skin is getting dry and gray."

He thought he'd hidden his physical changes from her.

"I'm fine," he said.

"You're not. We both know it."

Lyndon twirled a thick twist of pasta around his fork and pretended to study it.

"The problem is, I don't think you can stop."

"There's no reason to. Even the doctor said. I mean, I know it's cold, but my body can handle it."

"If you stopped, I think we'd both lose our minds."

"I don't think that's true," he lied.

"Yes you do," she said.

The next morning, he walked to the end of the dock. He watched his breath float away, a cloud in the cold air. He shed his towel and suit, and his testicles ascended close to his body. He jumped in. Everything felt perfect, and he slid through the dark water with speed and grace, maneuvering like a bird darting between branches. He glided underneath chunks of ice, coming up for breaths of air like a porpoise. He swam for hours and held delusions of swimming the length of the lake, though he knew better. That was impossible in a lake this size, a lake so large you couldn't take a speedboat across without stopping to refuel. Still, he continued on farther and farther from the dock, under larger and thicker blocks of ice, until he ducked under and couldn't find a place to surface.

He panicked, stopped, and turned his body in every direction looking for an opening. His chest tightened, and the water pushed in on him, squeezing him. He swam on skimming just underneath the sheet of ice, punching at it where it looked thin. Blood pulsed through his brain in heavy thumps, and his vision went blurry. He gasped and inhaled knowing this would be his death knell. Water filled his lungs.

His light-headedness dissipated. His vision returned. The pressure on his chest lifted. He took another breath and another. He reached up under his jaw line and felt tiny, almost imperceptible holes behind his ears out of which he expelled water. Gills. He filtered oxygen like a fish. He concentrated on the process of it, feeling the inhale and exhale.

Looking back, he'd been moving toward this for a while, but he'd been so set on ignoring the changes, he didn't appreciate his body's rapid adaptations. That desperate inhalation of water had been a necessary step, like the first fish to push up on its fins and walk out of the water.

Once he realized this, the sheet of ice above him became protective instead of restrictive. Above lay everything that'd proved difficult to navigate. He wanted to be exactly where he was, and he knew that if he stayed below a couple more weeks, the lake would freeze, "solid enough to drive your truck over," as the man at the tackle store had told him. All would be quiet, calm, like one long afternoon swim that stretched on and on.

He didn't like the idea of Heather looking across the lake wondering where he'd gone, the inevitable 911 call and search. He pictured tears streaming down her face as she stood on the dock. She still loved him, only things had gone awry at some point. Allowing Heather an end, to mourn his death, seemed kinder than continuing, than sitting across from her at dinner and eating in silence, letting her watch his skin grow scales, his hands and feet morph into fins. In time, she'd feel relief in his absence, an end to a stalemate.

In the deep, dark depths of the lake, Lyndon found schools of fish and rocks with crags and caves in and out of which he could dart. A new ecosystem. It would be lonely, but easy enough, simple. He chased a large scale sucker as it darted away, then moved to the shoreline and followed the contours of the rocks, the patterns of the downed tree limbs. He would learn this space, pick out landmarks and navigate his territory like he'd once done on land.

That winter, he swam, ate fish, learned the habits of the trout, the patterns of the sucker fish and the pike, where plant life grew thick from the sun, and where driftwood sank in deadened graveyards. He remembered his land life through fleeting memories of things like hiking through redwood forests or walking across warm Caribbean sands. Flashes of Heather mixed with these memories too: her bouncy curly hair, her smile, her high-pitched laugh. Sometimes he saw her older, sometimes younger, sometimes not visualized at all but remembered as background. She floated through his memories with an omnipresence in the same way water currents moved over his body. He remembered that before he'd slipped below the ice, he'd come to an impasse with her, that all had turned rotten, but he couldn't recall why, and it didn't matter anymore.

Lyndon hadn't anticipated the spring thaw, and the sound

of the ice creaking and echoing through the water surprised him. Fissures appeared, and Lyndon tried poking through in spaces. He surfaced and took his first lung-full of air since November. The air sat shallow in his mouth with his first few gasps, but with practice, breathing air became easier, more natural. His eyes, which had adapted so well to life underwater, did not work as well above it, and he had trouble seeing the shoreline.

Reaching his hand out in front of him, he examined his muted brown-green skin. Webbing stretched between the tips of his elongated fingers. He touched his face and felt the small bridge of his nose. His ears were now orifices rather than protrusions, and he'd lost his hair. He hoisted himself onto a sheet of ice and lay on his belly like a seal so that he could look at his reflection in the water. Big, round eyes, a flattened nose, a puckered frown of a mouth, a long sloping forehead. The gradual transformations had accelerated during the winter. Though he hadn't considered whether he wanted to return to life on land, already he wondered if he ever could.

Over the next few days, Lyndon made his way back toward the inlet in which his house sat. From the water, he looked up toward the deck and through the sliding glass door. At night, lights lit the living room window, and twice he'd seen Heather's silhouette.

Keeping vigil, he remembered when they'd begun dating and she'd pretended to like the Greek restaurant under his apartment because she knew it was all he could afford. He recalled an evening a few years ago, her smiling, green eyes growing wide in the glow of the fireworks after a minor league baseball game. He fantasized about going back in time to those moments, then looked down at his alien body, his scaly, muted-gray skin.

One warm evening, Heather walked out onto the back deck in her white nightgown. Lyndon watched her descend the staircase, floating like an apparition. She walked toward him and out onto the dock. Lyndon, afraid of being seen, ducked under the lake surface but stayed shallow enough so that he could see the wavy outline of her form shimmering through the translucent water.

She stood for a long time looking up at the gibbous moon, and the more he watched her, the more he allowed himself to think she thought of him. With sadness at least, maybe with fondness. How could she look at this lake each day and not think about his swimming ritual or that this lake likely swallowed and killed her husband? Why hadn't she left yet? Because she loved him. Because she also held on to memories.

He raised his head so that his eyes protruded above the surface. He studied the soft curls of her brown hair, the gentle lines at the corners of her mouth, her green eyes. She looked out across the water and didn't see him. The milky film obscured his vision preventing him from seeing in her face any sadness, remorse, or forgiveness. He tried to whisper, but the sound stuck in his throat. If he were to push it out, he feared it'd sound loud, coarse, and gurgled.

Instead, he reached his gray hand toward her and placed his webbed fingers gently on her toes. She flinched, pulled her foot away, then looked down. Their eyes met. She inhaled, giving her face a moment to contort into a grotesque expression, a pause of silence. Lyndon realized he'd miscalculated and anticipated her piercing scream an instant before she let it go. Her shriek carried over the water and echoed around the inlet. She dashed away, white nightgown fluttering behind her. With every step she took, it became less likely he would ever see her again.

His body felt heavy and awkward as he pulled himself onto the dock and lumbered after her. He yelled, but the noise erupted from his throat as a gnarled groan. She scampered up the stairway to the deck, looking over her shoulder with an expression of terror. Lyndon paused, wondering if he should continue. His skin felt dry, hot, and he longed to retreat to the lake, but this was his last chance at redemption.

He continued, using the handrail to pull himself up the

staircase. His webbed feet smacked against the wooden planks. By the time he reached the deck, he could hardly breathe and wondered what he expected to happen, what was the best possible outcome. Behind him, the lake seemed far away. He looked through the sliding glass door and saw Heather in the living room burrowing her face into Andy's flannel shirt.

Never, when deep in the darkness of the lake, did Lyndon picture Andy in his house. The scenarios he'd imagined, the possibilities for reconciliation, the fantasies of returning to a once-sound marriage, shattered leaving Lyndon with confused fragments.

Lyndon approached, hoping he could communicate to Heather in some way. He glimpsed his monstrous reflection in the glass, his hunched, scaly body. He tried to knock on the glass, but the webbing between his fingers prevented him from making a fist. Instead, his hand ran down the glass pane and made an eerie squeaking sound.

Inside, Andy pushed Heather away and ran into the bedroom. Heather stood there, hands to her face like Munch's "The Scream." Andy reemerged holding the shotgun, and he pointed it at Lyndon. He held it still, then hunched over and squinted as he looked through the scope. Lyndon took a step back. He looked at Heather and, knowing it might be his last chance, studied her face. He did his best to capture her image as well as her likeness: expressions, mannerisms, and movements.

The sound of the shotgun blast echoed through the house, the woods, and over the lake. Shards from the glass door sprinkled the deck like shrapnel. Lyndon fell onto the deck's wooden planks. His chest tightened up, and he couldn't breathe. The pain would come in a moment, and Lyndon wished that before it did, he could sink back into the water, a peaceful descent into the depths of the lake. They never should have come to Montana and shouldn't have let things progress down such a dark path once they did. Someone would examine his body when he died, maybe someone smart enough to realize who he was and what had happened. Heather would have to mourn all over again. Lyndon liked that idea because he had mourned his loss of her so many times. He'd lost her when his work days had grown indefensibly long. He'd lost her when they'd moved here. He'd lost her more when he'd started swimming. He'd lost her further when he hid underneath the ice all winter, and he was losing her for a final time as he lay bleeding about to die.

Lyndon rolled over on his side and looked at his webbed hand stretched out in front of him. So much had happened to him, but at the same time, he'd done so little to change course. He'd watched everything slip away, the ugliness growing. The webbed digits. The scales. The pool of blood extending outward away from his body along the wooden planks of the deck. He'd brought himself to this end, an end that might seem remarkable from the outside, but was in fact simple and common.

Heavy boots came into view in front of him. He lifted his eyes up. Jeans, leather belt, flannel shirt. Then, Andy's scowling face. He held the pointed, ornate end of a curtain rod inches from Lyndon's throat. Lyndon tried to look beyond him, to see Heather one last time, but couldn't. He turned his head and lowered his eyes back to the slats of the deck. Beyond the deck, in the distance, he could see the lake, the still water between the trees. An osprey circled. He took in this image and held it. One final look at the beautiful view.

Leo raised his arms to give the doctor access to his midsection. The doctor pulled Leo's shirt up and peered at the bright blue lump on his left hip near his belt line. "Well, the biopsy shows it's not cancerous." The doctor pushed on the lump. It slid to the side, then returned to its resting spot.

"It is quite vibrant, isn't it?" Leo said. At eighty-six-years-old, he'd let go of vanity. The color didn't look like a bruise but more like the bright blue color of lilies.

"Yes," said the doctor. He exhaled. "Sometimes, when the body reaches a certain age, things just crop up. I could refer you to a dermatologist."

Leo estimated the doctor to be forty years his junior. "No. Thank you."

"Well, we can at least try this." He scribbled on his prescription pad, ripped off a sheet, and handed it to Leo. "Topical cortisone cream. Apply it when you get home, then daily. A lot of skin blemishes clear up with this." Leo took the paper. He recognized the exchange signaled the end of their consultation.

He'd been prepared for cancer, a grave disease that'd already killed several of his friends. Three years earlier, his wife had died of heart disease, an injustice he felt because she'd been the healthy one, and he hadn't been prepared to outlive her. He'd expected his own death to come shortly afterward, but it hadn't. This growth on his side had no finality or severity to it which disappointed Leo.

He applied the cream when he got home. The next morning, when Leo removed his shirt to apply the cream to the lump again, it appeared larger and deeper in color. He put his shirt back on and looked in the mirror. Even clothed, the protrusion stuck out clearly.

Despite Leo's dutiful application of the cream over the next week, the lump grew. Leo speculated the cream irritated his skin, and he stopped using it. The lump grew still and extended down his hip and up around his lower back. He let his belt out two notches. The lump's color changed from blue to a vibrant purple, the color of rhododendrons, and stretched his skin making it shiny and glossy.

Leo's son came by and noticed it immediately through Leo's clothes. "Jesus, Dad," he said.

"The doctor said it's not cancerous," Leo said.

"Yeah, but it can't be comfortable," his son said. He wore a suit and was on his way to a dinner meeting in the city. He stepped closer, bent down. "What does it look like? Is it discolored?"

"A little decorum, please," said Leo, mostly joking but not entirely. He turned away.

"But, I mean, it's distorting your body. You can't even walk right."

His son was correct. He had to drag the left side of his body around to follow his right.

"You've got to go back, Dad."

Leo shrugged. He already knew how a doctor visit would play out. The doctor would knit his brow, write a prescription, or suggest surgery. He'd rather limp. Dying didn't bother him either, but explaining this to his middle-aged son seemed daunting.

Several days later, Leo sat in bed in his boxer shorts, the elastic band stretched to its limit. The lump extended down his hip to his knee, up his back, around front to his thigh and stomach. It glowed a dark, regal purple, like African Violets. He could feel the blood moving through it, a rhythmic pulse, and at the epicenter, its color and size waxed and waned with his heartbeat. Within the lump, Leo could see a pattern of concentric rings.

His son called and asked about the lump.

"It's fine."

"Really? It's gone down?"

"Well, no, but I'm not worried about it. It's not cancerous."

"Still, Dad, you don't know what it is. You could be dying."

"Well, I am dying."

"What?"

"Nothing imminent, just the usual natural progression of life."
He heard Max exhale deeply, then he said, "Dad . . ."

"I'm fine, son."

"Mom would have made you go to the doctor."

This was true, and he would have gone because he didn't like to see her worry.

That night, he awoke with a start to the sound of voice calling his name. He flicked on his light only to see the furnishings of his bedroom. Then, he heard it again: "Leo!"

The sound hadn't come through his ear canal as he initially thought. It simply entered his consciousness.

"Leo, it's me. That glorious lump on your side."

This, Leo thought, was a sure sign of dementia or schizophrenia, his brain growing soft like the rest of him to the point where he felt that the growth on his torso had begun communicating with him.

"I know you hear me, Leo. And yes, you have gone crazy."

Leo wasn't sure how best to respond. He thought to it, "What do you want?"

The lump sent back, "Greater consciousness, freedom, independence. What do you want?"

"To fade out gracefully."

"Maybe we can help each other."

"I don't know. There isn't a lot that's graceful about carrying a giant purple growth around on your body."

"I can be so much more than that."

"Like what?"

"A way out, for one thing. Unique, unexpected, magical."

"How do you envision this working?"

"Just leave it to me."

"It feels like I don't have much choice in the matter."

"Ha ha! Touché, Leo. Now, go back to sleep. We need rest."

"Is this relationship symbiotic or parasitic?" Leo asked.

"It's a matter of perspective. You choose."

The next morning, Leo stood in front of the refrigerator. The lump said to him, "No, no, no. This won't do. Start thinking protein, Leo. We're bulking up."

"I don't eat much meat. Barely eat at all, in fact."

"Steak for lunch."

"I don't feel like going out. I've got this large mass on my hip."

"Aren't you a clever bastard? Call the steak house. Have them use one of those delivery services."

"How do you even know that?"

"Because you know it. It's deep in there. Lucky for you, I'm climbing all over your brain, Leo."

Leo sat in front of the television eating a steak. He tried to remember the last time he'd eaten steak like that and thought back to an anniversary with Maxine. They'd read about some throwback K Street hangout, a place Nixon used to frequent, and gave it a shot. The whole time they ate, they made up stories about the beefy, middle-aged men in suits moving in and out of the bar.

"Admit it, you like that steak," said the lump.

"I do," said Leo.

"See, now you're living!"

"Eating like that will kill me."

"Leo, you die a little bit each day, but it's not everyday you truly live."

Leo rolled his eyes, then ground some pepper over his steak. "That is some true wisdom, Lump," he said.

"I stole it from you."

Soon, the lump extended out from his chest and back so that his arm simply lay on top of the growth. This, Leo realized, would soon happen to his other arm, then each leg, rendering him an enormous mass of swollen, immobile flesh. He did his best to lift his left arm but couldn't.

"This is what you call fading out gracefully?"

"Transitions are never easy. I am killing you after all."

"I don't want to appear grotesque."

"Oh, excuse me. Would you rather lose your mind slowly? Forget the names of all the people you care about? How about cancer? You can go through chemotherapy. Or, you can go on a breathing machine for a while. How does a catheter and bedpan sound? Your relatives can parade through and watch you deteriorate."

"I suppose you're right."

"Why don't we get you another steak?"

They ate like kings for a week. The lump asked Leo everything about his life from beginning to end. Leo remembered things he hadn't thought about in years, and he conjured up every face that'd ever meant anything to him. Finally, Leo could think of nothing else to say or to remember. He asked the lump, "Can't you go find all the memories in my brain yourself? Why did you ask me all of this?"

"To help you remember. Didn't it feel good?"

"It did."

"And have you been lonely since this began?"

"No. I haven't. For the first time since Maxine died."

"Are you seeing the grace in this now?"

"I am."

"Good. We're about done."

"I should call my son."

"Better do it today. You don't have much longer."

Leo couldn't move his left arm and leg any more. Flesh grew outward from his armpit illuminating the space between his arm and torso. He assumed the same would soon happen to his other arm. Next, his swollen left leg would grow into his right.

He dragged himself over to the kitchen, picked up the phone with his right hand, and dialed.

"Hello?"

"Hi, Max."

"Hey, Dad. What's up?"

"Just wanted to give you a call. See how you're doing. Did you see the Nats game last night?"

They talked for a while about the young pitching staff, the likelihood of a playoff run. Then, Max said. "Well, I'm kinda busy here, Dad. I'm at work, you know. Need anything?"

"Just wanted to say hi."

"Ok, I'll see you later, Dad. Everything okay? That lump?"

"Yeah, fine. I'll see ya."

He hung up the phone and let his hand sit there for a moment. The lump, respectfully, stayed quiet.

"That was it. The last time we'll speak."

"Most likely," said the lump.

"It wasn't so profound."

"There's substance between the words. He'll find it when you're dead."

"I hope you're right."

"I am."

"He turned out okay. He's a good man."

"Is there anyone else you want to talk to? Don't feel obligated. No one else knows this is your last shot. That's part of the grace I talked about."

"No, I think I'm done."

When Leo woke the next day, his limbs wouldn't move. With his head propped up on his pillow, he looked down at his body. His skin stretched tight. He'd become a giant, purple blob.

"I can't get up. Can't even eat."

"We're past that, Leo."

"It's time, isn't it?"

"Yes. Soon. I'll eat your brain too, and then your consciousness will disappear."

"I'm ready."

"Did I help at all?"

"It certainly was novel, and that's something."

"That is a rare something."

"And you helped me remember a lot." Leo closed his eyes.

The lump said to him, "You've had a good life, Leo. You've done mostly good, and you will be remembered fondly."

"You would say that to anyone."

"Yes, and anyone would believe it at a moment like this."

Silence. Leo felt his enormous body grow light. He pictured Maxine's smile, sometimes on a young face, sometimes on an older one. He saw Max as a toddler learning to walk. He felt his own child's body running through Shenandoah National Park during a family vacation and could smell the damp trees. He felt the sun beating down, pouring into him until everything washed out gracefully.

Candlelight flickered over the rusted handcuffs, leg irons, playing cards, jack knife, and fedora resting on the tabletop, and Eric, despite the promise he'd made to himself earlier to remain unaffected, felt a tingling in his stomach. The medium, Madame Boveen, chanted something incomprehensible, slow, and convincing.

Eric held Uncle Harold's left hand. His three bulky, gemstone rings felt cool in Eric's sweating hand. Out of the corner of his eye, Eric watched Harold's head droop forward, his eyes closed.

On his other side, Eric held hands with Dorothy Revnick, "the world's sexiest escape artist" of the late eighties, Uncle Harold's longtime "friend," and the source of Eric's most enduring adolescent fantasies. Dorothy's thin veiny fingers felt warm in his. He couldn't be sure, but he thought Dorothy's thumb moved ever so slightly back and forth across the base of his palm in a subtle caress. She wore a ring on each tan, orange finger, and she'd painted her perfectly shaped nails an impossible shade of still-wet red.

Three other magicians, friends of Dorothy and Harold, sat at the table. Eric had met them all years earlier and pretended to remember their names. They wore severe-looking suits. One had an impressive handlebar mustache.

The painted image of Harry Houdini peered down from the wall above Eric's head. The great escape artist stooped over, his muscled, naked body bound by chains, his head tilted up and his eyes peered out over the room. Underneath his image, bold red letters spelled out "HOUDINI!"

Houdini's widow had started the séance in 1927 at her husband's request and continued it annually for ten years on Halloween, the anniversary of Houdini's death. After that, other magicians and family members took up the cause. Uncle Harold, whose relation to the magician could only be explained by a generous examination of the family tree, and who'd served time for something no one would explain to Eric, had opened the Houdini Museum and started his own séance twenty-four years ago. The tradition spanned Eric's entire life. Once, Eric had brought a news clipping from the *Philadelphia Inquirer* to fourth grade show and tell. Even the name of the newspaper had sounded exotic to him compared to his parents' *Washington Post.* In the article, Harold expounded on the importance of the "grand tradition." The accompanying picture showed Harold in a double-breasted suit, his chin upturned and proud. Eric still had the clipping in a shoebox in his closet.

Madam Boveen, the hired spiritess, spoke clearly from her spot at the head of the table. "Houdini, if you can hear us now, make yourself known." She wore several colorful scarves over her wide shoulders and filled her ample leather chair. She closed her eyes and tilted her head toward the ceiling. Flickering candlelight danced over cracked ceiling tiles.

A week earlier, Eric had walked into the kitchen of his parents house, and his mom, on the phone, had exhaled and said, "He just walked in. I'll put him on." She pushed the phone into her blouse, looked at Eric, and said, "It's Uncle Harold. He wants you to participate in the annual idiocy."

Eric smothered a smile, took the phone from his mother, and said, "Hello?"

"Eric! It's Uncle Harold, and I've got the opportunity of a lifetime for you." He explained that Great Uncle Maury's death had opened a spot for a new family participant, that blood lineage meant credibility, and that Eric was old enough to know his history, to "feel the power of magic royalty that pumped in his veins."

Eric tried not to sound eager. "Yeah, ok," he said. Eric didn't believe in spirits, but he believed Uncle Harold to be full of mystery. Also, he was home after losing his first post-college job and needed purpose. Time away in a hotel, even one in central Pennsylvania, didn't sound bad either.

"Fantastic!" said Harold. "I'm glad I called. I thought, hey, if he's old enough to give the girls at college the business, he's old enough for the grand tradition."

The attempt at locker room camaraderie hit sour with Eric, mostly because he doubted Harold knew where he'd gone to college, that he'd finished last spring, or whether or not he was giving girls "the business."

After Eric hung up, his mom told him that while credibility through heredity makes for a better show, it also makes it harder for Harold's parole officer to deem the séance intentionally fraudulent, and that Harold was using Eric for his youth, naivety, and clean criminal record.

"Don't give him any money. Don't sign anything."

This made Eric want to go even more, made him want to truly feel his magical heredity. "I don't have any money anyway," he said.

"He's a morally bankrupt grifter."

"If he becomes financially bankrupt, that'd be a bigger problem, right?"

"Be safe. Be smart," she said. "Take my car."

When Eric pulled out of the driveway in his mom's Toyota Camry, he'd felt as if he were moving toward something important, something he'd been on path to do since childhood, something Uncle Harold knew he needed.

Madame Boveen waited for what seemed like an inordinately long time before speaking again. "Houdini, the great escape artist who amazed the world, escape again, Houdini. Escape the spirit world and meet us here."

Thirty Houdini fans had paid fifty bucks each to sit in folding metal chairs and watch an event that'd been free the year before. Eric couldn't make out the audience's faces in the dim candlelight, but he could see their feet. From the rounded ankles, slack cuffs, and dress shoes, Eric estimated them to be mostly over fifty, probably friends of Harold and Dorothy. Not a sustainable business model.

"Houdini, if you can hear me, please make your presence known."

Eric thought of the audience and wondered if he looked

austere enough. Did the spectacle itself look real or contrived and sad? He felt everyone's eyes on him and suppressed an urge to bolt out of the room. Beads of sweat ran down his forehead and made him itch, but he couldn't wipe them off.

"Houdini, you escaped chains, straight jackets, and torturous devices of your own design. Escape the afterlife and come to us now."

Silence. No one said a thing. Eric feared sitting there for eternity, sweating, watching Madam Boveen tilt her head toward the ceiling and sway back and forth gently, waiting in futility. Eric thought he felt Harold's grip tighten, though he could have imagined it just as he may have imagined Dorothy's sensual caress. He sat still, afraid to move. He became light-headed and worried he'd faint.

A crash upset the stillness, and before Eric could turn toward it, something heavy smacked the back of his head and pushed his face into the white tablecloth. He heard the sound of shattered glass spilling over the floor. The audience gasped, then murmured. Eric reached up to the back of his head, felt wetness, put his hand in front of his face, and saw blood. He looked down at the white tablecloth and saw flecks of red. He realized he'd let go of Dorothy and Uncle Harold, ruining the séance.

"Eric, you okay, dear?" Dorothy asked. She placed her hands on his shoulders. He turned to look at her and noticed the thick layer of powder on her cheeks. He turned around. On the floor, he saw the heavy, wooden-framed Houdini poster, the glass pane shattered.

Dorothy saw him looking at it. "It fell off the wall. The glass broke when it hit the floor, and then it fell forward onto your head."

Eric felt the heavy weight of Harold's meaty paw and bulky rings on his back. Harold stood and looked out at the audience. "Folks, we've obviously made contact. The great escape artist has escaped again. We must now attend to this young man."

Murmurs grew into loud voices as the audience shuffled

away. Eric caught pieces of conversations. "Is he okay?" and "Do you really think . . .?" and "staged," and "uncanny."

"We'll issue an official statement at a later date," Harold called out.

Harold placed his hand beneath Eric's elbow and guided him to stand. "Come with me, Eric." Harold led him past the large Houdini poster in its broken frame, glass shards littering the floor. Dorothy came from behind and took Eric's other arm.

Together, Harold and Dorothy led him through a backdoor into an office space he assumed to be Harold's. In the corner, he noticed an open toolbox with a screwdriver lying next to it.

Harold sat Eric down on a worn chaise lounge. Other séance participants filed into the room. Beyond them, famous magicians adorned the wall in a line of framed posters. Houdini, of course, but also David Copperfield, Criss Angel, and a younger Dorothy Revnick with big blonde bangs, ghostly blue eyes, and a ball of luminescence emanating from her long, perfectly red fingernails.

Eric's head pulsed. He listened to the voices around him. Uncle Harold cut through the mumbling and said to the group, "We've got to think now."

Madam Boveen said, "How bad is it? Should we call an ambulance?"

An older man in a long-tailed suit whose name Eric didn't remember said, "No, no. It's fine. No police," which surprised Eric because Madam Boveen had only mentioned an ambulance. The man with the handlebar mustache nodded in agreement.

Eric closed his eyes. His head throbbed. The crowd's footsteps sounded loud on the wooden floorboards. When he opened his eyes, he saw the poster of Dorothy again. From his spot on the couch, it was the only thing to look at without moving his head. Dorothy's blonde hair swirled about her in a hair-spray infused voluminous mass backdropped by misty pink and blue laser beams. She wore a short tux blazer buttoned low so that her breasts bulged out of the top. The jacket ended below her ribs showing her toned mid-section. A tight black skirt gave way to fishnet stockings. That's where the poster ended and it left Eric wondering what kind of seductive footwear she'd had on. How did she complete an outfit like that in 1988?

The real Dorothy behind Eric said, "Are you okay, dear?"

She sat on the arm of the couch and leaned over him to put a cold cloth on his forehead, her breasts inches from his face. Her perfume spread like a blossoming cloud and he looked down the front of her low-cut blouse. The unnatural orange color of her skin held true down to her black lace bra. He shifted his gaze to her eyes and in them saw the woman in the poster, the sexy escape artist of the eighties. Eric wondered if he could attribute this to blunt force trauma. She looked directly at him and curled her waxy lips on one side of her mouth. Eric thought maybe he'd been caught peeking down her shirt.

Uncle Harold's face replaced Dorothy's in front of Eric. "Are you doing okay?"

"I think . . ."

"It's important that we discuss exactly what happened. Obviously, you felt something."

"Yeah. That picture frame smacking my head."

"Before that. You felt him. Houdini. His presence."

Dorothy sat in an office chair a few feet away from Eric and leaned forward, eyes wide, the top of her cleavage showing at the neck of her blouse.

Eric said, "I don't know," which was soft pedaling it. He'd felt Harold gripping his hand tighter and tighter. He might have felt Dorothy caressing his palm with her thumb. He did not feel Houdini coursing through his body.

Harold exhaled and turned away. He got up, took a few steps away, then turned back toward Eric and adjusted his black opal pinky ring. "There's really no denying what happened. Everyone saw it. The thing to do is to come up with a statement. People are going to want to know what you experienced."

"All I remember is being in there with you guys and being kind of nervous with all those people out there looking at me . . ."

"There must be something special about you though," Dorothy interrupted. The inflection of her voice moved up and down melodically, a sweet interjection to Harold's gruff tone. "I mean, after years of his wife doing the séance, his family, his friends, and he found you." Her blue eyes shone bright from her cavernous, heavily painted eye sockets. Eric stared at her long mascaraed eyelashes.

"I don't know," Eric said.

"Sure, sure," she said. "I just know it." She walked over to him and put her hand on his chest. It made him want to sit up from his reclined position, but he knew it'd be too conspicuous a reaction to what was probably an innocent gesture. He'd sexualized her nurturing unfairly, a woman his mother's age.

Uncle Harold, pacing the room, waved his hand dismissively. "How about this: we say you're recovering from your injury. We'll issue a statement to the media tomorrow."

"There's media?" asked Eric.

"You sleep on it, and we'll come up with some quotes to put in the press release."

"I don't like the limelight, Harold. Isn't that your job? I mean, for the museum and everything?" he said.

"You sleep on it," said Harold. "You may change your mind."

Eric shrugged. Dorothy smiled at him. Harold's friend in the long-tailed suit peered out the window at the street. Madam Boveen looked down at the floor.

Eric lay on top of his garish bedspread in the Red Roof Inn and flipped through channels on the TV. He heard a knock on the door, opened it, and saw Uncle Harold. "Eric. I'm sorry to bother you, but we've got some things to discuss." He pushed the door open, walked in, and sat at the small, heavily lacquered table near the window. "Please sit," he said motioning to the chair opposite him. Eric flipped off the TV, then squeezed past the bed and sat opposite Uncle Harold.

"Now, I don't want you to say anything. I just want you to listen."

"Okay."

"The thing to remember is that people want to believe the unbelievable. They need magic and magicians. That's part of what I do. It's part of what our family does, and it's where your first name comes from. Tomorrow, you're gonna have a choice about whether you play into that or whether you make this séance, this museum, just some hokey roadside attraction. You have a chance to make magic, Eric, and I want you to remember how much people need that."

It had never occurred to Eric that his name came from Houdini's real name, Ehrich Weisz, and he couldn't tell if Harold had made this up. Harold's eyes looked wide and sincere. He twisted the black opal pinky ring on his left hand. His thick, gray eyebrows arched upward and he smiled. Eric got the sense he'd heard the one true thing that Harold held onto, the one piece of morality he'd retained over the years.

"Also, I'd like you to sign this statement. It's short, but important."

Harold took an envelope out of his inside jacket pocket and unfolded a paper with a short, typed statement confirming that Eric "genuinely believed he'd made contact with the soul of Harry Houdini."

"Harold, I can't . . ."

"It's simple. Just eases up some of my legal problems. Makes it hard to paint as a fraud. You know I had a run in with the law a few years back. You can do that for me, right?"

Eric didn't speak. Harold slapped Eric's knee too hard, then stood up. "We'll talk more tomorrow, okay?" Harold moved toward the door leaving the typed paper on the hotel room table. Harold looked down toward the ground, and Eric saw a tear forming in the corner of Harold's eye.

"Bye, Uncle Harold."

"See ya, kid," he said, and then left.

Eric went back to the bed and flipped through the channels on the TV some more, but couldn't attend to any one show. What Harold said made some sense, but it didn't fit with what Eric wanted, why he'd come in the first place. He wanted to flee back to D.C., to get out of this whole situation and find a job, a real job where he had to wear a nice shirt.

An hour later, he heard a knock on the door. He figured it'd be Uncle Harold again or a hotel employee saying there's a problem with Harold's credit card. Eric went to the door and opened it a crack. Dorothy smiled at him through the narrow gap. She'd curled and expanded her hair into a display of grandiosity. Her floral perfume, which carried visceral undertones of mysterious scents like wet leaves, mist, and a muddy creek bed, floated through the doorway.

"Can I come in?" She stood waiting, biting her lower lip, and this made Eric consider the weight of her question, if she wasn't asking for more.

"Sure," he said and opened the door. She wore a short skirt and black stockings with a subtle textured pattern. Fishnet? Fishnet meant sex, didn't it? Hadn't she stroked his hand with her thumb? She stopped and looked at the bed where Eric had laid his black suit out flat on the comforter.

"You should hang that up," she said.

"I will," he said.

She took off her jacket to reveal a sleeveless red blouse, the top three buttons undone. She laid her jacket across the back of a chair. He thought again about the poster of Dorothy in the museum, her firm breasts highlighted by the neon backdrop. He did the math and as best he could figure, Dorothy was between fifty or fifty-five, at least twenty five years his senior. This might be generous, but he felt like being generous. The woman on that poster didn't exist anymore, but in his head everything blurred together and time bent. In the Red Roof Inn in central Pennsylvania, reality didn't apply. He wanted the woman from the poster with the firm, sleek midsection and high cheekbones, the sexiest magician of the eighties.

She fixed her blue eyes on him and stepped forward as if she were on stage about to address an audience. Eric froze. Dorothy came closer and put her hand on his shoulder. Her red bra strap peeked out from the neckline of her blouse.

"I know you're special," she said.

He smiled. His heart beat fast.

"You are, aren't you?" she said. She tilted her head to the side as she asked it. He couldn't speak. She moved closer and put her hand on his chest over his t-shirt and looked at him with the same deep, mysterious eyes he'd seen on the poster. He felt the warmth of her breath on his lips. Her perfume swirled about like an extravagant cloud. "Houdini chose you. After all these years, he chose you, because you're special. There's something about you, something coursing through you. Something powerful, don't you think?"

She moved her hands down to his waist and gripped the sides of his torso. He put his hands on her hips as well, though he knew she could tell he was uncertain, scared. She whispered in a breathy tone, and he bent closer to her mouth to hear it. "What did it feel like? Tell me what it felt like." As she said it, the tips of her lips brushed his earlobe. Goose bumps shot up on his forearms.

He should push her away. She was old, his mother's age, Uncle Harold's girlfriend he'd known since childhood.

"Hard to explain," and when he said it, he felt her move back slightly.

"But you felt it, right? You could tell he was there with us, right?"

"Sure," he said.

She came back closer, then rested her head on his chest. He smelled her citrus shampoo.

"I knew it," she said. "You're special, Eric. Remember that. Tell them tomorrow."

"Okay," he said.

She walked over to the table where Uncle Harold had left the statement and pen. She brought it to Eric. "You need to sign this," she said, "to let everyone know." He did. She exhaled, pulled him close, then took his hand and led him to the bed. She pushed him gently down onto his back. Then, she straddled him, her skirt pulled tight across her parted legs and riding up so that he could see her thighs in her black, fishnet stockings. She undid his belt. The metal buckle clacked in a loud, unmistakable sound announcing exactly what was about to transpire.

"You're special, Eric. That's why I'm here. Don't forget that. Remember it tomorrow, when the cameras are on, the reporters." She tugged on the waist of his pants. He lifted his hips to help her.

"Okay," he said.

She reached for his penis. "When they ask you tomorrow, you tell them, right?" she said.

"Okay," he said.

Her blue eyes sparkled from their cavernous sockets. She kissed him with her waxy, painted lips. Eric closed his eyes and saw neon laser beams.

Eric sat alone at the same table they'd used for the séance only this time the well-lit audience consisted of two cameramen and three notepad wielding reporters. "Not so many reporters," Uncle Harold whispered in his ear, "but one is from the AP so the story could spread." Harold walked from Eric's side and joined the audience in a chair next to Dorothy.

The Houdini portrait that'd knocked Eric in the head sat on the floor behind him, shattered glass still strewn about. Specs of blood dotted the floor. He wondered if Harold had doctored the scene, flicked a paintbrush loaded with red over the floor.

Uncle Harold stood up and turned to face the reporters. "Let's get started, shall we? Thank you all for coming. For decades, our family has followed Harry Houdini's, Ehrich Weiss's, dying wish that we try to make contact with him in the afterlife. Last night, the famed magician reached out to his namesake, Eric Jefferson, in dramatic fashion. I will turn it over to Eric now."

Uncle Harold motioned toward Eric with his ring-laden hand and sat down. Dorothy smiled at him, her blue eyes sparkling underneath prodigious eyelashes. She looked older than she had the night before. The lines at the corners of her mouth ran clear and deep.

Eric read from the paper Uncle Harold had printed that morning. "Last night, on the anniversary of Harry Houdini's death, being one of Houdini's few remaining direct decedents, I took part in the one-and-only Official Houdini Séance here at Harold's Houdini Museum. While others have been performing this ritual since the magician's death in 1927, this was my first time taking part. Not long after we started, I felt something unique and terrifying, something like a bolt of electricity shooting through my body."

Eric looked up at this point to see if anyone would stop him and call bullshit. No one did. Dorothy's thick, glossy lips spread wide. Harold looked at him sternly and nodded.

"It felt like Harry Houdini had entered my body. It felt like nothing I've ever felt before." Eric paused, about to deliver the line he found most objectionable. "It felt . . . magical."

Harold nodded in approval. Dorothy's red nails slithered up Harold's knee. She slid her fingers between Harold's. Eric saw a speck of red paint on the back of Harold's hand. For the first time, Eric noticed the black opal ring on Harold's pinky matched the ring on Dorothy's pointer finger. Dorothy rubbed her thumb slowly up and down Harold's thumb.

Eric completed Harold's script. When the small pool of reporters called out questions, Uncle Harold jumped up and said, "That's it for now, folks. We have copies of Eric's signed statement, and we're happy to pose for pictures. Dorothy and I can answer questions about Houdini and the museum."

A camera-wielding reporter pulled on Eric's arm and guided him next to Dorothy and Harold. Harold put his arm on Eric's shoulder. Dorothy sidled in on the other side. She bent her knees and pointed her hips at the camera. Her orange-tanned cleavage pushed out of her blue, sequin top.

Once the reporters left, Harold and Dorothy walked him into the room with the chaise lounge and the poster of Dorothy. Eric exhaled. Dorothy turned and looked up at him with her large, sunken eyes. "Thanks, babe," she said, and she stood on her tiptoes and kissed his cheek. He wiped his face with the back of his hand removing a mass of red lipstick. Behind him, Harold cackled loudly, then slapped him on the back. "If you want a job, Eric, you could hang around here, ride this out, make a nice go for a couple months."

"Yes, but after a while you'd need a new gimmick," Dorothy said.

"That's true," said Harold. "We could turn you into a kind of medium. You could do well with that. Only it'd have to be your own thing. I've got . . . conditions to abide by according to the state."

"That why you needed my signature?"

Harold shrugged.

"What about all that stuff about feeling the power of magic royalty pumping in my veins?" said Eric.

"Well, that was me playing to your desire for grandeur. Still, you could make it true, put it in the papers and on TV. The Great Eric Jefferson!"

Eric looked around the dingy room. A thin layer of dust covered the picture frames on the wall. The museum smelled like an old closet, or more aptly, he thought, like the inside of a coffin. Uncle Harold would likely die here. Maybe Dorothy too. He pictured a queen-sized bed in a back room with black satin sheets and playing card pillows, Dorothy's fishnet stockings on the floor next to Harold's wingtip shoes, matching rings on opposing night stands.

"I gotta go home," said, Eric.

"Stay a couple days, Eric," Dorothy pleaded. She sounded sincere which surprised Eric, yet he wondered if this was the continuation of an act, if this was her still toying with him for Harold's amusement. Despite everything, he almost wanted to stay. He was ankle deep in thick mud and sinking fast. If he didn't pull his feet out now, he'd get stuck, and that had some appeal.

"I need to find a job," Eric said.

Uncle Harold huffed as if he'd said something funny. Dorothy and Harold walked Eric to his mom's Camry which he'd parked behind the museum next to Harold's '88 Cadillac.

"You know," Eric said, "I only came here as a favor to mom. She said you needed help."

"Well I did, and I thank you," said Harold. He bowed deep as if concluding a performance. "Dorothy seems to think you had some fun here nonetheless." He winked.

Eric hurried into the car. Before leaving, he took one last look at Harold's museum. He noticed chipped cement around the base of the foundation and a gutter rail hanging askew.

"See you next year," said Harold.

"I don't think so" he said.

"It's in your blood," said Harold. "You can't escape family. It's tighter than a Houdini straight jacket."

"Then I will astound you," said Eric.

"This is the most astounding thing you've ever done, Eric. A great illusion. You think of that while you're wearing a tie stuck behind a desk."

Harold and Dorothy turned around. Eric watched the sway of Harold's pinstripe suit, Dorothy's gait in her stiletto heels and tight leather skirt. Harold put his thick hand on Dorothy's hip, his rings sparkling in the sunlight. They were the saddest and most incurably magical people Eric would ever know.

Aree's Abstract

"To encourage spots and blobs he tugs the ear forward, towards the canvas. So, very sadly, the design the elephant is making is not hers but his. There is no elephantine invention, no creativity, just slavish copying."
— Desmond Morris, Daily Mail, February 21, 2009

Aree watched her mahout approach: his long metal hook resting on his shoulder, his gnarled, leathery face pinched in a scowl. He grabbed Aree's ear and led her past a young elephant tied up between four wooden posts. Dried blood covered the elephant's face, and his trunk hung low. As the mahout passed, he swung his hook in a lazy, half-hearted motion striking the elephant on his back. Aree had been "broken" like this too long ago. She turned her head away so as not to lose resolve for her planned insubordination.

The mahout led Aree through the bamboo forest which shrouded her grim accommodation from tourists. Next, they walked down the tunnel, one side clear plastic glass, the other side a cinder block wall wheatpasted with prints from Van Gogh, Munch, Picasso, Klimt, Hopper, Homer, and others. Aree once had a young mahout who'd talked about those paintings as he lead her down this chute, a daily, 100-yard art education.

The tunnel opened up into a larger paddock. Aree approached the easel set up there and faced the steel-cable fence and the tourists beyond it. The mahout grunted and handed her a paintbrush loaded with black. She hated the necessity of this, that despite her aspiration and talent, she wasn't physically able to pick up a paintbrush without human help.

Aree heard the familiar low-level chuckle from the audience. The mahout tugged her ear. A small nail hidden in his palm dug into her skin and guided her to the starting point on the canvas.

She painted the same thing every day: two elephants trekking through a field of flowers. She used simple, representational outlines for the elephants, short brush strokes for grass, and specs of color for flowers. The mahout's hook hovered above. His nail tip pinched the back of her ear and guided the arc of her lines.

Aree recognized the paintings on the cement tunnel wall as comedy through juxtaposition. How many human painters were there? She assumed many. Only a population rich with artists would laugh at the folly of an elephant trying her hand at this lofty human endeavor. Extrapolating from the small sample of human work she'd seen, she imagined a near infinite number of artistic styles and longed to create something of her own.

Aree had never seen a field of flowers like the one she painted daily. Her compound was raw and dusty. The captive elephants imprisoned with her wore their plight in the form of complex, wrinkled, scarred, and fragmented faces. Deep, severe lines. Picasso's cubism mixed with the dark outlines of Van Gogh's trees.

The mahout tugged down on Aree's ear, a signal for her to complete the downward slope of her subject's trunk. Instead, she closed her line to make a small rectangle. The mahout mumbled, then smacked her back with his hook. He tore the paper off the easel and hung a fresh sheet. He grunted, reloaded the brush, handed it to her, and pulled her ear hard, his nail digging into her skin. Again, Aree began the slope of the trunk, then made the sharp right angle of a rectangle. The mahout struck her three times.

She wanted to paint a piece that showed the depth of her experience. She'd already composed it in her head and needed materials and space to realize her concept.

The mahout reached to tear off the paper again, and Aree swung her trunk and pushed him out of the way. He stood back wide-eyed looking at her from shoulder to toe as if noticing her enormous size for the first time. She added several more lines, the amalgamation of rectangles began to form an elephant face refracted and reimagined. The mahout yelled and raised his hook high. Aree kept painting and stomped her foot twice hard and heavy. The ground shook. The mahout quieted. The crowd gasped. She reloaded her brush and made dark, heavy lines.

The mahout approached from the side. She turned to face him, and while instinct told her to trumpet a great sound of warning, she didn't want to drop her brush. Instead, she grunted and made a sudden move with her head as if she were about to charge. The mahout froze giving Aree more time with her canvas.

She worked furiously knowing others would soon rush in, beat her, sedate her, or dole out whatever punishment deemed appropriate for an elephant breaking from realism and delving into abstraction. She didn't have time for the self-critic. Instead, she marveled at the waterfall of shapes spilling down her paper, hard edges that together made the gentle slope of an elephant's trunk. Her subject's eyes looked wise and hard between her clean, angular lines. She heard murmurs from the visitors beyond the fence but stayed focused on her work.

Then, out of the corner of her eye, she saw seven men approaching. They carried rope, hooks, a dart gun, and an electric prod. If she could finish painting the head and face of her portrait, that might be enough. A few simple lines suggested the outline of the body already.

The men surrounded her. She stepped back and looked at her canvas. In it, she saw all her influences — the posters she passed daily, her life experiences — and she was satisfied. Next, she felt a jolt of electricity shoot through her.

She'd once heard a trainer say an elephant has 40,000 muscles in its trunk, and she thought how this elaborate interwoven systems of nerves and small muscles had to be more complex and nuanced than human fingers. In those 40,000 muscles Aree imagined potential for new techniques, new brushstrokes. Now, with the pulse of the electric prod, her trunk muscles stiffened, and she dropped her brush. A sharp pain pierced her neck and she turned to see a man lowering a dart gun. A moment later, the tranquilizer took effect. Her legs gave out. She sank to her knees, and her vision blurred.

A man threw a canvas bag over her face. With much effort, Aree lifted her head and pushed the bag from her eyes with her trunk. She took one last look at her work. Her mahout took the paper off the easel and looked at it quizzically. Then, he tore it in two, the sound an audible end to Aree's experiment in abstraction. She gave in to the tranquilizer and let her head fall back to the ground. She wondered if there were any artists behind the steel cable fence with enough empathy to understand what she was feeling.

Five Feet Eleven Inches

Karen noticed the thinning hair on the top of Sam's head, and the image captured her attention to the point that she couldn't focus on what he was saying. She'd never seen him from that angle before. When Sam left the kitchen, Karen stood on her toes testing her height in her sneakers and trying to remember exactly what part of the refrigerator should be at her eye level.

She'd gained several pounds recently too. In response, she ate less and jogged three times a week, even though it meant picking up Ashley later from daycare. After a few weeks of this regimen, she decreased one notch on her belt but didn't cut weight. Also, her shoes felt tight on her feet.

Without saying anything to Sam, she marked her height against the closet door and found she'd grown a full inch and now stood five feet eleven inches, a half-inch taller than Sam.

After noticing this, she said to Sam across the kitchen table, "Sam, I feel like I'm growing." He put down the newspaper, sat silent for a moment, then said, "like pregnant?"

"No," she said, surprised by the disgust in her voice. "Like height growing."

He tilted his head. "Why do you think that?"

His calm demeanor could be aggravating. "Fuck if I know, Sam." She told him about the weight gain and the shoes too. She took him upstairs and showed him the marking inside the closet door. They talked in whispers because Ashley slept in the next room.

"See?" she said, pointing at her mark on the inside of the closet door.

He took a book and pencil from the nightstand and motioned for Karen to stand against the door. She did, and he put the book on top of her head and made a mark. She stepped away and saw his mark just above her recent measurement. Then, he moved toward her so that their noses almost touched and ran his hand over their heads. He stepped back and furrowed his brow which creased his face and reminded her how long they'd been together.

Six Feet Five Inches

During the examination, the doctor wouldn't look Karen in the eye. If he'd tried, he would've had to angle his gaze upward. Afterward, he left Karen and Sam in the waiting room, then reemerged twenty minutes later and led them into his office.

He walked behind his large, mahogany desk, motioned for her and Sam to sit, and sat down in a wingback chair. Sam scooted his chair close to hers and held her hand, a gesture Karen found both belittling and endearing.

"It's likely abnormal activity in the pituitary gland," the doctor said.

"Is it harmful?" Sam asked.

"Usually, when excess growth hormone is introduced, harmful changes occur."

"Usually?" said Sam.

"As far as I can tell, Karen is perfectly healthy," said the doctor. He looked at her and smiled, exposing gleaming white teeth.

"Why is this happening now?" Karen asked.

He shrugged. "Sometimes the body reacts physically to emotional stressors."

Karen shrugged back. "Like cataclysmic emotional events?"

"Yes."

Both the doctor and Sam looked at her intently. "No," she said. "Nothing like that has happened." Sam leaned back in his chair. "But . . ." Sam's head turned toward her quickly. "What about maybe smaller things?"

"What do you mean?"

"Like nothing. Nothing's happening, and my body is trying to wake me up?"

The doctor sat up straight and skewed his eyebrows. "I don't understand."

"My body is forcing change instead of reacting to it?"

"I suppose that's one way of looking at it," said the doctor. He looked down at his desk and scribbled something in a notebook. "The important thing is that you appear healthy."

"Can you stop it?" she said.

"In most cases, it's caused by a tumor, and we operate. You don't have a tumor."

"You can't stop it?"

"Well, there's not really anything wrong with you. Growth in adulthood is abnormal, but your growth plates have opened up, your bones are healthy. Everything's fine."

"I'm fine?"

"Well, yes."

Sam turned toward her and smiled. He put his other hand on top of their already clasped hands. She pulled her hand away, then looked back at the doctor.

"Is there anything else?"

He shrugged again. "You can go."

She got up quickly. Sam followed her out and called from behind her, "Karen, that's good news. Good news, Karen!"

Seven Feet

She ducked under the doorway of the daycare center. Ashley's teacher forced a smile and said, "Good afternoon, Karen." The teacher turned toward the group of kids and called, "Ashley, your mommy's here." Ashley turned, her blue eyes wide, and stared at Karen. Her blond pigtails stuck out and accentuated her expression of surprise.

"Ashley, it's mommy," she said. Ashley only tilted her head. The silence hit Karen in the stomach. Then, Ashley's stare broke. Karen felt the muscles in her neck and shoulders relax.

"Mommy!" Ashley yelled, and she ran into Karen's arms. She picked her up and held her against her chest, squeezing her thick thighs and thanking her silently. On the drive home, they sang along to The Rolling Stones.

Seven Feet Three Inches

Karen turned the business card over in her hand and ran her thumb over the Boston Celtics logo.

"You should at least consider it," Sam said.

"It's stupid."

"It could be fun."

"I don't think so. Plus the travel."

He shrugged. Ashley played on the floor between them organizing plastic animals on the living room rug. Karen knew if she left for too long, if Ashley saw her growth all at once instead of daily, her daughter wouldn't recognize her.

"If you don't want to do it, I understand."

"Seven foot three isn't that tall for the NBA, is it?"

"WNBA then. And you could get taller." He said it like it was an uncertainty. Then he said, "It is a lot of money, though. The first woman ever, too. Wouldn't that be something?"

"It would be something."

"I mean for Ashley. Her mom the first female player in the NBA?"

"I don't like basketball, Sam."

"This is bigger than you."

"Few things are bigger than me."

He smiled, and she did mean it as a joke, but not entirely. He came over to the couch and sat next to her. He leaned against her shoulder. If she moved away, she'd have to explain why, so she stayed. They hadn't had sex since she'd surpassed him in height nearly three months ago.

"I'm going to start a load of laundry," she said, and got up.

Seven Feet Six Inches

The nurse led Ashley to the scale. She stepped onto it, her head down, her toddler belly pushed out against her pink t-shirt. Karen knew she was about to cry but the nurse didn't. "Thirty-two pounds. You're getting to be a big girl," said the nurse. "Let's measure you." She led Ashley over to the ruler mounted on the wall. "Stand up straight," said the nurse. Ashley did. With her chin up, Karen could see Ashley's watering eyes. "Thirty three inches," said the nurse. "If you'll just wait in that room, the doctor will be there in a minute," she said motioning to a small examination room.

They entered, and Karen sat on a plastic chair. Ashley, her face in her hands, climbed into Karen's lap and began sobbing. "What if I get too big, Mommy, like you, and the doctors can't make it stop?"

Karen stroked her back.

"Oh, honey, that won't happen to you Ash," she said. "I promise it won't." But Karen had no way to know.

Eight Feet One Inch

"It's fine. It's your decision." He lay flat on his back, the covers pulled tight across his chest, a position he never used for sleeping.

"I don't want to go down that road," she said. After the letter from the Celtics, there'd been calls, emails, and letters from World Wrestling Entertainment, Universal Studios, daytime talk shows, and several publishing houses.

"I understand."

"Maybe it'd be different if I'd always been tall, if I'd grown up with it."

He didn't say anything. She turned toward him, but couldn't see his expression clearly in the dark, only his profile.

"I know you're right. It's just . . . you could make a lot of money, Karen, especially now that you're not working."

"We'll get by."

"We're gonna need a bigger house."

"It could stop," she said, but she didn't believe it. What she thought more likely was that by the time they found a new house and lined up the financing, she'd be too enormous for any house at all. Not to mention the grocery bills.

"It could," he said, then rolled over pretending to sleep.

Eleven Feet Four Inches

She held Ashley against her chest and bent her head down so that her lips brushed the top of Ashley's blond curls. She inhaled and smelled the remnants of the clean baby smell that, at age three, she hadn't quite lost. "I love you, Ash," she said. Ashley squirmed in response. "What's the matter, kiddo?" Karen asked. She pulled her face away from her daughter's so as to read her expression clearly.

Ashley's lip contorted into frown. She looked down. "Too high, Mommy. Too high!"

Thirteen Feet Six Inches

"Sleep in the bed," she said. "I want you to get some rest."

"I want to be next to you."

They lay on the floor underneath several blankets, which together, covered Karen's length. Sam scooted close to her and nuzzled into her armpit. He reached his arm across her belly in an unmistakably platonic way.

"This isn't going to work for much longer," she said. She'd propped her pillow against the wall, and her toes almost touched the opposite wall of the bedroom.

"Let's not talk about it right now."

"I'm going to need to leave."

"Where will you go?"

"You won't want me here much longer."

"I love you, Karen. We'll make it work."

"Christ, Sam." She rolled over so her back faced him. He pulled his arm away. She began crying but held her lips tightly so she didn't make any noise. Still, her sobs made her shake. Sam began stroking her shoulder. She scooted away further taking most of the blankets with her. She heard him exhale deeply and turn over.

Thirteen Feet Eight Inches

As Sam put his keys in the front door, Karen stood hunched between the kitchen and the living room holding the package she'd found on the doorstep. The return address read California Bodies, LLC, and the Internet showed they sold everything that claimed to make you bigger.

He walked through the door and let his work bag fall to the floor in the foyer. "Daddy!" said Ashley, and she ran to him and gave him a hug, her small arms reaching to his shoulders when he bent down to her. "I'm watching Dora, Daddy," she said.

"Oh yeah?"

Ashley scrambled back to the couch. Sam stood up again meeting Karen's eyes as he did so. Karen saw her stern look reflected back at her through his worried eyes.

"What?"

"This came today," she said holding the box toward him. She shook it gently. It rattled. "Some kind of pills? California Bodies?"

His look told her she'd caught him at something. She raised her eyebrows to invite an explanation. He walked toward her, his eye level near her belly button, and talked in a hushed tone to keep his words from Ashley. "I needed to do something, to have some control."

"What's in here?"

"I felt I was losing you," he said, looking up at her and reaching out to touch her.

She stepped back. "What's in here?"

"Pills, Karen."

"What kind of pills?"

"Growth hormone."

She shoved the box into his chest. He took it, retreated back into the living room, and placed it on the coffee table. He sat down next to Ashley and put his arm around her. She leaned in close to him, and he kissed the top of her head.

Eighteen Feet Ten Inches

Knowing Sam would arrive soon with Ashley, Karen pushed the hay into neat piles in the corner of the warehouse behind the beer stills. She brushed the hay out of her hair with her fingers and smoothed the skirt that Jackson, the brewery owner, had made for her out of burlap sacks. She straightened her black Capital Brewery T-shirt. Contractually, she had to wear it at all times. Regardless, it was all that fit her.

She heard the squeak of the door. Sam led Ashley by the hand, but as soon as Ashley saw Karen, she burrowed into Sam's leg and reached her arms high signaling she wanted to be picked up.

He obliged, then said, "Ash, it's Mommy. See Mommy?" He pointed at her. Ashley turned into her dad's shoulder.

"Ash, come on. Say 'hi'," he said. He turned his body trying to position her to face Karen.

"It's okay, Sam."

"Ash, just say hello. Your mommy loves you so much, Ash. She just wants to see you."

Ashley began kicking her legs.

"It's okay, Sam," said Karen.

"I don't know why she's doing this. It hasn't been that long, and we talked about it in the car."

"It's okay, Sam. Stop."

"She still loves you Karen," he said.

"Okay, Sam. Okay."

"I still love you, Karen."

"Stop it."

"I do."

Ashley's whimpering grew into crying, then shrieks. "DAAaaady, DAAaaady!"

"You look like you could use a beer," said Karen. Sam laughed. He laughed so hard he began to cry too.

"It's fine, Sam."

"I still love you, Karen."

"Just shut up, Sam."

"You're not saying it back."

"Just stop."

They stood there awhile, Ashley still screaming. Karen said, "It's okay. Go home. Maybe try another day."

Sam nodded, and they left. Karen took the top off a barrel

and drank, though her contract expressly forbade it.

Approximately Twenty-Nine Feet

Sam put in the DVD and set up the LCD projector so that it shone on the wall of the warehouse. Pushing buttons and twisting dials had become too difficult for Karen.

She sat on a pile of hay and hugged her knees, her head a few feet from the rafters. Sam sat on her left kneecap. Looking down on him, she saw the white of his scalp through his brown hair.

"Are you sure you want to watch it?" he asked.

"It'll be fun."

"Okay," he said. He patted her knee.

The ominous music began. The title came up: *The Attack of the Fifty-Foot Woman.*

Karen liked the simplicity of the plot line and wished she felt the same rage as the film's gigantic protagonist. She could throw cars and destroy the city. She looked at Sam sitting there on her knee. She thought about pinching his head between her fingers, picking him up, and tossing him out the window. That's it. Done.

Before he left, he said, "I love you, Karen."

"Don't say that anymore, Sam."

"It's true."

"You shouldn't come here anymore."

"You don't love me?"

"I'm tired."

"I know it's hard, Karen."

"You don't know."

"You're right. I mean, I can't imagine . . ."

"I'll tell you, it's ridiculous. Insurmountable."

"Nothing is insurmountable."

"Then tell me where I'm going to live next," she said and pointed up at the ceiling.

He patted her knee, and she thought how easy it'd be to squeeze his head until it popped. "Thanks for the movie," she said.

Approximately Thirty-Seven Feet

She found a can of red paint in a closet and spread out several sheets of cardboard she'd taken from the dumpster by the loading dock. Her index finger just fit into the gallon can. When she pulled it out, it looked bloody. She did her best to write small.

Dear Sam,

I'm leaving. It's unlikely I'll be able to disappear, but please know that I would if I could. I know things will be tough for you and Ash, and I'm sorry. You don't see it yet, but this is the end. Don't come after me.

She looked over what she'd written. Callous, but it stated things clearly. After spending time deliberating over how to sign the note, she wrote:

With love, affection, and fond memories,
Karen

A closing appropriately backward looking.

She took a barrel of beer from the storeroom and drank it, something she did frequently now. There wasn't much her benefactor could do about it, and without a barrel of heavy stout daily, she couldn't ingest enough calories. She grabbed six more barrels and a dozen loaves of bread, wrapped them in her spare t-shirt, tied it into a ball, and slung it over her shoulder.

She bent down and inspected the sliding loading dock doors in the back of the brewery. Like the oversized Alice, she'd become too large to fit out the way she'd come in. Placing both hands against the support beams of the roof, she pushed open a large section, then climbed over the wall, careful to step around the cars at her feet.

Approximately Fifty Feet

Helicopters, most covered with TV station logos, others painted a pea-green military tone, buzzed around her like houseflies. King Kong, she thought, acted out of annoyance more than viciousness when he swiped at those biplanes.

Karen sat on the bank of a small river, her knees bent to form an archway over the water. She leaned against a rocky embankment and sipped on a barrel of beer. The treetops swayed erratically in the wind from the copters. Still, the sun shined, and Karen felt comfortable in her Capital Brewery t-shirt. It was September. The weather would hold for a few more weeks.

A Park Ranger emerged from the forest holding a clipboard. He looked up at her, cupped his hands to his mouth, and yelled, "Excuse me!"

She turned toward him.

"Hi. If you want to be here, in the park, you need a permit to camp. Do you have a permit?"

She looked up and watched the slow progression of the clouds while trying to ignore the helicopters.

"Excuse me! You're going to have to leave!" he said.

Karen looked at him, slowly raised her left hand over his head, and held it there. It cast a shadow over him, and he stood staring at it wide-eyed. His stern expression broke, and he took off running into the forest. A pea-green helicopter swooped down toward her. She raised her hand to shoo it as she would a fly, then realized the severity of her gesture and put her hand back in her lap.

Several hours later, a Channel Seven copter set down on the riverbank. The rotors spit dust into the air, and she shielded her eyes with her arm. The helicopter left, and when Karen took her arm away from her face, Sam stood on the rocky beach, a cameraman behind him.

"Hi," he said. He wore a suit and held a bouquet of red roses at his side.

"What are you doing?"

He shrugged. His face sagged in embarrassment. "I wanted to see you."

"Who's he?" Karen said, gesturing to the cameraman.

"They want to do a TV show. They got me past the barricade."

"There's a barricade?"

"National Guard."

"Oh." She sat up and peered over the treetops trying to spot the military presence. Then she said, "Did you see my note?"

"Yeah, but . . ." he looked toward the river for a while, then turned back toward her and said, "Ashley misses you, too."

"I can't go back."

"I know."

The cameraman crept behind Sam and used one hand to hold the camera, the other to nudge Sam's hand holding the flowers.

"Oh. These are for you," he said, holding up the roses.

"I'll run and get a vase from the pantry."

He set them on the beach.

"Nice suit," she said.

"Yeah, they bought it for me," he said. "Look, I don't know what to say. I just wanted to come."

She noticed hair on the back of his hands and assumed it was a side effect of the growth hormone. If he'd grown at all, she couldn't tell. Then, gesturing to the cameraman, she said, "Good money?"

"You know that's not why I'm here."

"I wish it were."

"Yeah, me too."

"What do you tell Ashley?"

"That Mommy had to move away. That we still love each other, but that you just got too big. That's true, right?"

"Things weren't perfect before," she said.

"Marriage takes work," he said.

She nodded.

"So, can I still come see you?"

"At some point, the work isn't worth it. It's just done."

"How do you know when? When did that happen to us?"

"At about thirteen feet, sleeping on the floor in the bedroom but knowing it wouldn't last much longer."

"That's when you knew?"

"Yeah."

He picked up a pile of rocks from the beach and began throwing them into the river one at a time. Then, still facing the water, he said, "I didn't know. I didn't know this morning."

"Well, now you do."

"What's going to happen now?"

She shrugged and looked up at the helicopters swirling above. "Maybe I'll lash out and see what happens." She turned back toward him, "Tell me about Ashley."

"She misses you."

"Other stuff. Good stuff." A tear fell from her cheek. She caught it with the back of her hand.

"She likes cows now for some reason. Everything cows. I think she saw one on the milk carton, and now she carries her plastic cow everywhere and holds it up and moos."

Karen smiled. "Cows? Really?"

"Yeah. This weekend I'm taking her to some touristy farm. They're having a milking contest."

Karen smiled. "You're a good dad, Sam."

"Thanks," he said, then threw a handful of pebbles into the river.

"I'm running out of food. Even in the brewery, they couldn't keep up with my appetite."

"Well, you're not exactly wasting away."

She lifted her shirt on one side exposing her clearly visible ribs.

"Oh." His face melted into a look of severity.

"It's okay, Sam."

"What are you going to do?"

"Well, I was going to jump off something but couldn't find anything tall enough."

He looked at her horrified.

"Sorry," she said.

"It's okay."

"So, cows, huh?" she asked.

"She loves cows."

They sat together, neither speaking, until the cameraman

approached Sam, his camera at his side. "Um, excuse me. My producer wants you to kiss her hand or something."

Sam looked startled. Karen said, "It's fine, Sam." Then, she turned to the cameraman and said, "We can do better than that. How about a full-on lip smack?" She carefully positioned herself on all fours straddling the river, her chin resting on the riverbank next to Sam, and puckered her lips. He stood on his tiptoes, his face aligned with her enormous mouth, and kissed her.

"Perfect," said the cameraman. He put down his camera and said to Sam, "Okay, we're done." Then, he called for the copter on a walkie-talkie.

The copter touched down on the beach. Sam looked at Karen. She nodded in response, then watched him climb into the helicopter. It ascended and headed east toward the city, toward Ashley, getting smaller and smaller. She'd never get over losing Ashley, but watching Sam recede into the distance, knowing the National Guard would keep him away, made her feel good. She picked up the barrel of beer and took a swig. The alcohol started to soften things. She extended her legs and leaned back against the riverbank. Even with the helicopters buzzing overhead, she had some solitude. It'd been years since she'd been alone this way.

Marisa's brown eyes shone bright as she walked toward me and curled her lips in a slow smile. I smiled back through a dull haze of beer and Jack Daniels and took a long look at the tattoos blanketing her arms from the tips of each finger to the sleeves of her form-fitting black t-shirt. In this newfound intimacy, I'd earned the right to stare.

She stood on her tiptoes, wrapped one hand around the back of my neck, placed her other hand on my hip, and pulled my face down to hers. Her lips pushed hard against mine. I inhaled. She smelled like vanilla and leather. I wrapped my arms around her thin waist, so small and slight, and wondered how this body had withstood the tattooist's needles over and over. I slid a hand over her bob haircut to the buzzed nape of her neck.

"Sit down," she said, and pushed my chest gently. I sat on the edge of the bed. She went to the light switch, and I wanted to stop her, tell her to leave it on so I could see every clue inked on her body, all the images so long hidden from me beneath her clothes. I imagined a sculptor taking a cloth off his latest creation in a grand unveiling, and this idea, more than her kiss or the curve of her neck under my hand, fueled my lust.

For months, she'd run my groceries over the scanner at checkout while I stole glances at her tattoos. Vonnegut's "so it goes" ran along her forearm. One of Louis Wain's psychedelic cats perched on her bicep. An inked ring broken by a dark, jagged line decorated the fourth finger of her left hand. A reproduction of Frida Kahlo's "The Wounded Deer" ran along her tricep. Fresh red ink punctuated the arrow wounds in the deer's body. How old was Marisa? I saw the beginnings of crow's feet at the corners of her eyes.

"You like Vonnegut?" I'd asked pointing at her arm.

"Yeah. One of my favorites," she had said without looking up, still moving my items from the conveyer belt to plastic bags. A shallow response to a simple question. Three weeks later, I asked her out.

She flipped the switch off, but the streetlights from 14th St. shone through her cracked curtains, and once my eyes adjusted, I could see the images on her body again. Walking toward me, she peeled off her shirt and dropped it to the floor revealing a large flying saucer on her chest just under her clavicle. Tractor beams shot from the bottom of the UFO toward each breast and disappeared into a black spandex bra. The beginning of this new story, so close to me, so unexpected, made me want to rip her bra off to see the next chapter, the trajectory of the tractor beams.

She pushed me down on my back and straddled me. I stared at the spacecraft. The luminescence of her pale skin made the shining light from the saucer's portals glow.

She caught me looking and said, "I was abducted once."

I couldn't tell if she was joking. She pulled at my shirt, and I lifted my torso so she could get it over my head.

"By aliens?" I asked.

She laughed and said, "That word can mean several different things."

I didn't know which word she meant, "alien" or "abducted." I ran through the possibilities.

Alien: 1) A little green man. 2) A foreign national. 3) Unfamiliar.

Abducted: 1) Taken aboard a spacecraft by little green men. 2) Physically removed from a location. 3) Figuratively removed from a mental state of being.

Was she crazy? I should have used the term "extraterrestrial." That would have cleared things up. I wondered about a troubled childhood, abuse, or neglect leading toward sadism or delusions of an alien abduction. Was I taking advantage? Was I even capable of pleasing her sexually at all? What was I to her? How old was she? Was she white or Latina?

She got up and removed her pants, and I got a quick glimpse of tentacles wrapping around her torso and her hips, a pirate ship under siege. Before I could finish admiring all of the images and colors, she straddled me again. She straightened up and pulled off her bra. A swirl of black dots circled the nipple of each of her small breasts, marking the end of the tractor beams. On her right breast, the tractor beam held the small body of a girl in silhouette, limp-bodied, mouth agape. A dog floated in the tractor beam on her left breast.

"Your body is amazing," I said.

She laughed and said, "I know."

She pulled my boxers to my thighs, and started moving her hips back and forth, her pubic hair and labia brushing the tip of my penis over and over. I lifted my head and stared at the octopus on her hip, the way it wrapped around her torso, one tentacle moving right to the edge of her vagina. On her shoulder, a bigfoot lurked behind a row of trees, full moon overhead. She caressed her breasts with her hands, and again I focused in on the broken ring on her left hand. What kind of pain did she carry?

My penis grew harder, aching. Still, I wanted to stop her, turn the lights back on, because after months of wanting to know more, this could be my only chance. I didn't know how to change course, and she kept moving, gyrating over me. The gentle brushing of my penis escalated to grinding, and I could feel her wetness on my shaft. I couldn't speak, couldn't move, and couldn't determine if I even wanted to disrupt this anymore. This woman, this creature, was unlike anyone I'd ever met, otherworldly with impenetrable mysteries. Her hands pressed down on my chest. She lowered herself down and pulled my penis into her as if with a powerful tractor beam. I tilted my head back, my mouth open in a silent moan, the same posture as the girl above her right breast. I gave in, focused on the sensation, the ecstasy, resigned to the fact that she would remain alien to me, that I'd never know everything, and trusting that after she finished with me, I'd be set down safely again on earth.

Theodore Carter is the author of *The Life Story of a Chilean Sea Blob and Other Matters of Importance* (Queens Ferry Press, 2012). His fiction has appeared in several magazines including *The North American Review, Pank, Necessary Fiction, Potomac Review,* and *Gargoyle.* His street art, which began as a book promotion stunt, has appeared on TV. and in print in several Washington, D.C. media outlets.

Acknowledgements

My wife, Elizabeth Carter, read all of these stories in early drafts and many that did not make it in here. I'm grateful for her input and consistently honest criticism. Jeremy Trylch did much the same, and I'm grateful for all he's done to help me grow as a writer. My mother, Alice Carter, also provided feedback on several stories. Thank you to Courtney Granner for the fantastic cover, and to Gary Anderson and everyone at Run Amok Books.

Most of these stories have previously appeared in small magazines and anthologies. Behind each of these outlets are talented, creative people working hard to champion the work of others. That's remarkable and commendable.

I'm thankful for the art, myths, and histories which supply me with constant stimuli and enthusiasm for the world we create together. And, if you're a reader and made it all the way to the end of the book and are even reading this, you're pretty great too.

"Final Notice" first appeared in *Well Told Tales*; "Shorebird" first appeared in *Necessary Fiction*; "The Thirty-Ninth President and the Fourteenth Tentacle" first appeared in *Stupefying Stories*; "Frida Sex Dreams" first appeared as "Frida Kahlo Sex Dreams" in *North American Review*; "Teddy Wins" first appeared in *Gargoyle Magazine*; "Escape from the Menagerie" first appeared in *THEMA*; "Devotion" first appeared in *Corvus Magazine*; "On Hokusai's The Pearl Diver and the Octopus" first appeared in *Black Scat Review*; "The Creature from Flathead Lake" first appearead in *Kaaterskill Basin Literary Journal*; "Lump" first appeared in *Surreal Grotesque*; "The Great Escape" first appeared in *Second Hand Stories*; "Aree's Abstract" first appeared in *The Ekphrastic Review*; "The Fifty-Foot Woman" first appeared in *PANK*; "Abduction" first appeared in *Le Scat Noir*.